From the Ashes

Book 3 of The Ember Files

Shari Marshall

Writing Sparkle Books
sharimarshall.ca
Alberta, Canada

Marshall, Shari
From the Ashes: Book 3 of The Ember Files

eBook ISBN 978-1-7782531-8-8
Paperback ISBN 978-1-7782531-7-1

Fiction | Fantasy | Urban
Fiction | Fantasy | Humour
Fiction | Fantasy | Contemporary

This book contains a short story from *The Ember Files* series.
Marshall, Shari
A Prick of Magic

eBook ISBN 978-1-7782531-6-4
Paperback ISBN 978-1-7782531-9-5

Dedication

Dedicated to you; thank you for all your support. And dedicated to me for not only penning a book but writing the series through to the conclusion.

From the Ashes

Chapter 1

Fin bursts into the living room, hollering my name. A chemical scent similar to nail polish remover wafts into the space with her. Grama Pearle pauses with the rim of her coffee mug touching her bottom lip, her mouth quivering with a smile. "It must be time for the unveiling," she whispers.

Fin calls me again, her voice animated. Her electric green eyes are as round as saucers, and her normally well-kept, shaggy black bob appears like she was teasing it backward with a comb. She's so thoroughly covered in splotches of acrylic paint that I wouldn't be surprised if she were naked, wearing painted-on clothing. Even if she didn't resemble a madwoman, Fin wearing paint as clothes wouldn't surprise me.

"Have you slept, Fin? Not to mention fed or watered yourself?" I ask with my eyebrows hiked nearly to my hairline.

She takes a second to focus on me, and I feel sure that my nut job friend hasn't slept. My life's motto pops into my head as I watch her: *When crazy calls, Kori Ember answers.* It's not as sexy as my best friend and roommate Finley Salinger's motto, though. More often known as Fin, her motto involves dark stallions, sparkling unicorns, and insatiable appetites.

"Kori," she groans like I'm raining on her parade, but she doesn't answer my questions. She's holding a thirty-five-by-thirty-five-inch canvas behind her. "After days of being locked in my room, I've created the symbol for us, The Influencers." Her smile stretches across her face. "We can hang it in Just Flavours, wink, wink."

I know by her not-so-stealthy code of "wink, wink" that she doesn't mean the restaurant itself, but the control centre she built. Fin and I actually live in an apartment above Just Flavours, the small restaurant Fin and Belamey Adelgrief own. Just the thought of Belamey, as is always the case when I think of him, causes my nerve endings to stir and tingle with yearning.

When Fin and Belamey renovated Just Flavours nearly a year ago, Fin had the restaurant decked out with magically warded clandestine exits and a well-concealed operations room for those days when missions get complicated. Missions are one of the ways I've come to terms with my unusual life.

Just over two years ago, I accepted a job from a man known to the majority as The Recruiter, but known to a select few, including me, as Cian. A man who lives a secret and guarded life and collects the best Spellbinders to work for him, keeping the Spellbinder world safe. This is also how Fin's arts and crafts project was born.

Last year, we found out that The Society of the Blood Wind has a unique red symbol for their evil organization and its power. Two long, sideways flames stacked one over the other—representing far-reaching hands—cup several faded swirls emblematic of wind being released. Fin took it upon herself not only to come up with a symbol for those of us who work for The Recruiter, but to name us as well. Our title, The Influencers, evolved from a bit of friendly banter between Fin and Belamey. Satisfied with coming out on top of the repartee, Belamey has taken no interest in image creation.

Fin, versatile to a fault, is the first normie to join Cian's team, and she takes pride in her role. She's a rare normie, no longer bound by conditioning that impedes the ability to perceive magic. Since Fin's conditioning faltered, she sees magic by conscious choice. Maybe conditioning for normies is self-inflicted, or maybe there's a history there; I don't know, and I've no desire to seek the answers. The fact of the matter is they are conditioned and perhaps always have been.

Although Spellbinders and normies live amongst one another, normies don't know about the world of magic that surrounds them. They limit believing in magic to stories, fairy tales, myths, and legends. They make sense of magical things they refuse to accept by explaining them away as superstition, coincidence, and scientific reasoning.

"My masterpiece is ready. I went abstract with it, simple but abstract. Are you—" The sound of our apartment door opening and two men's voices mingled in conversation interrupts Fin.

"Hush!" she thunders at Belamey and Dodo as they walk into the room carrying takeout bags from Just Flavours. "I'm ready to reveal."

Belamey and Dodo exchange a look, suggesting Fin is often ready to reveal things. Dodo, while becoming more and more like his mentor Belamey every day, won't be so bold as to make a comment. Belamey, not constrained by those same inhibitions, questions Fin with his husky voice. "And what, dare I ask, is your risqué exhibit today?"

Fin blows him a kiss, which is short for kiss her ass. With that, she flips the canvas from behind her and tips it so we can view her artwork. If my eyes were going to come straight out of their sockets, this would've been the time. My mouth hangs open, and I'm taking long, drawn-out blinks, hoping the image will change into something other than what it appears to be.

Fin's head is down, and she's admiring her work from that angle. "I wanted eyes to represent our watchfulness, but not normal eyes, so I created these." She swings her hand down and up the canvas. "And this is a pointing finger. My way of saying we always get our man or woman."

Fin's alleged pointing finger is aimed straight up and she's positioned it between the so-called eyeballs. I close my mouth and swallow before I trust myself to speak faint enough that Fin won't hear. I whisper to

Grama Pearle out of the corner of my mouth. "Is that what I think it is?"

Grama Pearle gives a whoop. "Hot dog, Fin, can you paint me one of those?"

I whip my head in Grama Pearle's direction.

She's licking her lips and rubbing her palms together. "It reminds me of—"

"Blazing hell, don't finish that sentence," I say louder than I mean to. Flustered, I gaze around.

Dodo is bright red and scanning the room for something to focus on.

Belamey moves close to me, still eyeing Fin's painting.

Fin, staring at Grama Pearle, is bouncing in place. "You bet I can make you a copy, Grama Pearle." Fin turns the canvas and lifts it to eye level so she can inspect it presumably a second time. "I—" She lowers the canvas fast and gapes at us like she's just seeing the likeness of the image for the first time. Subconsciously painting a sexual image is something she'd do. She yanks it back up, blocking her face from sight.

Belamey nudges me. When I turn to peek at him, a wicked grin crosses his face. "How are your artist skills, Firecracker? I'd be willing to be your nude model." Between Fin's painting, Belamey's use of his nickname for me, and his offer to get naked, my lady bits are feeling feverish, and the warmth is spreading over my body. I'm struggling not to pant.

Fin's voice is high-pitched behind the canvas. "The eyeballs I painted resemble stylized abstract breasts and the finger . . ." Her breath hitches. She moves the canvas downward. Her voice is soft and halting, like she can't believe what she has created. "The finger has the appearance of a beautiful penis!"

The corner of Belamey's mouth twitches, but before he can comment, Grama Pearle hoots and starts hopping as if she's riding a horse while smacking her behind. Fin is staring dumbfounded at her artwork, and Dodo is trying to escape by tiptoeing toward the front door. Nobody but me notices his getaway, and I don't point it out because I appreciate the desire to avoid this ridiculousness. I recognize my need for calm amongst this chaos and whip my chakra stones out of the pocket of my studio pants.

The stones have just begun to hover over my palm because of the air currents I'm manipulating when the window by the sofa bursts open. Most of the stones clatter to my feet, missing my palm, when I release the currents to arm myself with orbs. These spheres, which vary in size, serve multiple purposes for Spellbinders, including defensive magic that now comes to me without effort.

But my orbs don't form because I identify the indigo bunting that swoops into the room through the open window. It's Belamey's mother—Rye or Astrid, depending on the day and the role she's playing. Grama Pearle believes Rye is dead, a ruse necessary for both their safety. She doesn't know that Astrid and Rye are the same person. None of us knew until about six months ago when Rye revealed her secret while helping us—The Influencers—with a mission Cian assigned us.

I flick my eyes in Grama Pearle's direction without moving my head, but I hurry to refocus on the bird because I don't want Grama Pearle to notice my discomfort. Keeping Rye's secret from Grama Pearle is distressing.

Rye just clears the window frame as she shifts, landing on her human feet in a cattish crouch. She's wearing her Astrid persona. Her clothes are dishevelled, her spikey ashen hair is unkempt and almost flat, and her light brown eyes are wild, scanning the space. When her eyes land on me and Belamey standing shoulder to shoulder, she stands and drops her disguise. She becomes her true self, Rye—a modest change.

"They've taken him!" Her voice is raw with emotion and anguish, with fear at the forefront.

My eyes scan her, taking a closer note of her state. I can detect a faint odour that's both metallic and sweet; her clothes and skin are spattered with patches of blood in various states of drying. I tip my head and sniff deeper. There's the unique stink of a death orb, an acrid, honeyed stench reminiscent of an electrical fire. None of the blood appears to be Rye's, but her level of exhaustion has her wobbling on her feet. Belamey is already at her side, his arms stabilizing and comforting her.

On top of what I'm sure was a fight for her life, she's had to travel a long way to reach us. The last time Belamey, Fin, and I spoke to her, she and Cian were travelling to an undisclosed location on the other side of the world. Assuming Belamey would be here, she would've travelled to find him without stopping. He's the only other person with whom she feels safe or loved. My brain is in overdrive. *The Society of the Blood Wind has to be behind the abduction; it has to be.*

Fin is scurrying, laying out a sheet and pillow on the sofa.

"They've taken him," Rye repeats, her voice fading as her body gives out.

Belamey scoops her up and places her on the sofa.

"Rye?" Grama Pearle's voice is breathy. She's been speechless until now, no doubt trying to put together how a woman she thought dead for decades could be standing in front of her.

Rushing past us, Grama Pearle shoves Belamey out of the way like his six-foot-two athletic build isn't an opposing force to her five-foot-one, hundred-pound frame. She bends low to peer at Rye's pained but sleeping face. She strokes Rye's cheek, and I note the faint stream of brown and green magic feeding from Grama Pearle to Rye. It's Grama Pearle's special way of soothing people. The creases of concern in Rye's face soften, and her breathing settles.

Grama Pearle wheels on us. Tears glisten in her eyes. She locks each of us with a pointed stare, assessing where to lay the weight of her words. "You," she says, pointing at Fin.

Fin lowers her head, her cheeks colouring. "I'm sorry, Grama Pearle."

"I'm hurt by your silence." Grama Pearle switches her stare toward me.

I glare back, silent.

"How could you, Kori? I keep more secrets than any other person." Her voice drops off. The pain of us withholding this from her is heavy, even though it wasn't a secret for anyone but Rye to share.

She turns from us and sits on the edge of the sofa, taking Rye's hand into hers. "Leave us," she whispers.

I swallow and look at Belamey. His eyes are sympathetic as he watches Grama Pearle with his mother. He nods and turns, following Fin when she heads into the kitchen. I move to the open window and close it before I use the air currents to draw my chakra stones to me. Once they're all nestled in my palm, I hurry out of the room, leaving Grama Pearle and a sleeping Rye to their privacy.

Chapter 2

Fin has cleaned herself up and made coffee. Belamey, Fin, and I are standing in the kitchen, staring at our mugs in silence when Grama Pearle enters the room. I lift my eyes, but not my head, from my cup of coffee.

Grama Pearle has stopped just inside our modern kitchen with her feet planted wide. There's a tightness around her hazel eyes as she takes a minute to assess each of us. Her deep, cleansing inhale and exhale of air is the only noise in the room, and then she physically shakes herself. I watch as her shoulders drop from their uptight position and the tension drains out of her.

"Coffee, please," she says, climbing up on a stool at the breakfast bar. Grama Pearle waits for Fin to slide a mug into her hands before she speaks. Her tone doesn't reflect any of the emotion I expected to hear, but her words convey enough. "I'm hurt. That statement is for all of you." Her hand flies up in a *wait* gesture.

I don't check, but I'm sure we're all frozen with similar words on our tongues.

Grama Pearle continues. "I'm hurt, but I understand this secret wasn't anyone's but Rye's to tell. Now isn't the time to get into details about Rye. What matters now is keeping each other safe and finding Cian."

She lifts her coffee to her lips, her eyes flickering with her thoughts.

"The Society of the Blood Wind?" Fin blurts out. She shivers, her eyes wide. "Hold on. Did I mention that a strange young man was lingering outside of Just Flavours a few minutes ago when I glanced down?" she says, pointing to the window.

Grama Pearle is closer than I am; she hops off the stool, charges the window, and pops her head out and then back in. "He ran." She sounds surprised.

I stick my head out the window, scanning in both directions, but the sidewalk is empty. Pursing my lips, I pull my head back inside. I close the window and face Fin. "What did he look like?"

Fin wiggles her nose, and for a second, I'm worried based on her dramatic nose movement that she's going to compare his appearance to a smell. "A fucker. He looked like a fucker!"

Grama Pearle points at Fin. "Yes, he did! And not the kind you wanna bring home on a Friday night. Discreditable, a bad seed, trouble oozing from his pores."

They both ignore the glare I give them in response to

their very unhelpful description.

"Kyson," I announce with confidence, deciding there's no point in dwelling on who might or might not have been on the sidewalk. "Kyson took Cian."

Grama Pearle's head moves down and up once.

"He'd send a message." Belamey's husky voice startles me.

The mention of a message makes me think of Kyson's last words to us a few short months ago when he said, "Our time will come and with it, each of your deaths." His grating words—an oath to the dead Dolion, as much as a threat to us—was a promise to kill us all. He has motive because not only does he blame us for Dolion's death, but we also killed Kyson's twin.

"The message will come soon. Kyson's waiting to make sure we're all in one place. He wouldn't miss an opportunity to build terror and flaunt his . . ." Belamey struggles for a word, and his voice is tinged with anger. "Victory." He slams his fist on the counter, making us all jump. "We've been waiting for him to pounce. How the fuck did we miss this?"

Belamey doesn't wait for a response. Spinning, he storms from the apartment.

"We never expected an attack on Cian and Rye. As targets, we seemed obvious. Cian only gives the orders. He wasn't even there when Kyson threatened us." Fin scratches her head. "Should we . . ." Fin swallows. "Go after Belamey?"

I shake my head as I stare in the direction Belamey disappeared. "No, he'll be back to speak to Rye." I refocus on Fin.

She scrunches up her face. "You don't think he'll go searching for Kyson?"

My gaze drifts to the doorway, and my words feel mechanical. "There's been no movement at The Society of the Blood Wind house since Dolion's death. Maybe Kyson is their leader now, but we have no proof of that."

"But Kyson is Belamey's cousin. They grew up together." Fin is shaking her head no, answering her own question while she's asking it. "You don't think Belamey has an idea where Kyson might be holed up?"

She continues speaking her thoughts out loud. "Belamey is our man. That horrible grandfather of his, Mister I'm-So-Mean Dolion Adelgrief, tried to kill Belamey. Kyson is a psycho who lives to kil—"

Horrified, she gapes at me, then at Grama Pearle before staring toward the living room where Rye is still sleeping. I know she's struggling with her fear for Cian's life and the crushing impact it will have if he's murdered. Fin swallows, "Belamey better hurry. We need to find Cian."

As if on cue, Belamey bursts into the apartment with Dodo in tow, bringing the faint odour of sugar and fried dough with them. *Dodo must have been cooking fresh donuts for the specialty breakfast sandwiches.*

"Nobody should be alone," Belamey says, nudging Dodo into the room.

Dodo straightens his lanky body and casts his dark eyes in the direction of the living room. He surprises me when he moves across the room, opens the window, and whistles. He addresses us without turning to face us. His voice is soft but purposeful. "I'll send messenger birds to anyone we think is in Kyson's crosshairs. And don't worry, I'm up to date on who those Spellbinders might be."

Movement in the living room distracts any of us from responding to Dodo. He stays at the window calling pigeons to send messages while we hurry to see Rye.

She's sitting up on the sofa now. Her expression is pained, but she schools it, and a steely glint enters her eyes. "Pearle," she breathes. Standing with open arms, she moves forward. Judging by the length of time they embrace, it's clear both women are trying to maintain control of their emotions.

When they step back, Grama Pearle rests a finger against Rye's lips. "There's no need to explain any of that, Rye. I'd have done the same to protect the ones I love." Grama Pearle's manner hardens. "Now, tell us about Cian."

Rye's head shakes, and she says nothing. We watch her and wait. Head still shaking, she manages to say, "I don't know." Her eyes move over each of us. "I went out to get fresh fruit for a fun honeymoon breakfast. The braying sound of a blue-footed booby caught my attention, so I looked up for the source of the bird call. I saw them leaving our condo as I was on my way back."

Fin's sharp intake of air is startling. "You two are powerful Spellbinders. You'd be difficult, if not impossible, to beat together. They didn't want to risk losing to two Spellbinders when they outnumbered you. So, they waited for you to leave, putting the odds in their favour." The pitch of her voice is increasing as her thoughts build to make her point. "This attack was a power move. It's conspicuous, ballsy, and a threat toward the overall Spellbinder power dynamic. Taking Cian is a powerful message."

Belamey stalks toward Rye, "Who's them?" The wisps of magic that I normally see attached to his person are pulsating from their usual thin threads to thick, glowing strands. The predator in him is dying to hunt.

"I saw a red-tailed hawk. So, Kyson, for sure. There were four other birds. One crow, a marabou stork, a blue-footed booby, and some kind of vulture. I think the vulture was a cinereous vulture, based on its size and the bluish-grey skin on its head, neck, and legs." Rye's jaw clenches.

For a moment, I'm worried that she's clamping her teeth together hard enough to shatter them. It seems like she has no control over the tension in her jaw, and she's forcing the movement of her mouth.

"Cian was in bird form . . ." she pauses, "in a net carried between the stork and the vulture." Her eyes squint with anger and her nostrils flare. "He wasn't moving."

I can hear Fin mumbling what might be names and bird types. I'm shocked that there was no classic Fin comment about the booby bird. Grama Pearle must hear Fin too because she looks at her and gives a nod and a flick of her hand.

I don't know if the flick is meant to silence Fin or shoo her from the room.

"Hm?" Fin says, tipping her head to the side and considering Grama Pearle.

Grama Pearle ignores Fin and reaches for Rye's hand. I think she's going to soothe her with calming magic, but no threads are visible. They squeeze each other's hands and close their eyes. Rye's voice quivers with her next words. "If they could overpower Cian, I knew I had no chance of defeating them alone." Her eyes open.

Grama Pearle opens her eyes too and moves so she can peer straight at Rye. "You made the right choice. Cian wouldn't want you in danger. We're your family, Rye. You don't have to fight *this fight* alone." Grama Pearle places her hands on Rye's shoulders and turns her into Belamey's waiting arms.

"Wait," Fin says, her eyes moving between each of us. "The net holding Cian was magical, right?"

"Do you remember the elastic handcuffs that pair with Griffin's belt buckle when we captured Adria Blaze?" Rye's voice is muffled by the position of her head on Belamey's chest. She doesn't wait for Fin to respond. "These nets used to be used by the Allurist Detention Centre for capturing and moving Spellbinders being transferred into their care. They have physical and magical components. The prison board deemed the nets too harsh a treatment, and the prison stopped using them. The Allurist Detention Centre stored them but didn't destroy them. I don't know why. And yes, that means that the one used," her voice quivers, "on Cian would have come from the prison. Another unknown for us to puzzle over.

"Anyway, the net works in a similar way, controlling Cian's magic and ability to shift. If the net is coupled with a buckle, then the proximity of the two is important because the net will constrict around whatever it's holding the farther it gets from the buckle, with the potential of killing whatever is inside."

Grama Pearle turns her gaze to Fin, lifts her eyebrows, and flaps her arms. This is her second attempt to hint at Fin to do something.

Fin's eyes flash wide as she catches on to what Grama Pearle wants. "The crow would be Blake, without a doubt, because Kyson was mentoring him. Remember, Belamey told us that Nekane, who is burning in hell, assigned that poor, impressionable Spellbinder to Kyson for training." She's yelling over her shoulder as she runs out of the room.

The muffled sounds of papers rustling, items banging, and drawers being opened and slammed filter out of Fin's bedroom. "YES!" she hollers, and her feet thunder our way. She slides into the room, holding my younger sister Alivia's sketchbook up like she's carrying a first-place prize. I hadn't realized that Fin still had the sketches. I haven't seen her with the book since the Ember stone was returned to the rock trolls.

"Those birds sound familiar, but I want to make sure, so just give me a few minutes to flip through Alivia's drawings and notes of Spellbinders and their birds." Fin plops down on the sofa. "I'm sure those birds are in here," she mumbles.

Grama Pearle glances at Rye and Belamey. Rye has recovered enough that she's standing on her own beside Belamey. Grama Pearle scrutinizes me.

"Kori, with Rye's permission, using your Memory

Keeper skills here would be beneficial."

I pull back, shocked. "Why me? Why not you?"

Grama Pearle raises an eyebrow at me.

Fin doesn't look up from the sketchbook in her lap. "Because, doughhead, Grama Pearle's emotions from the shock of Rye being alive after all these years might not allow her to pick up helpful stuff from Rye's memory. Right, Grama Pearle?"

"Good insight, Fin." Grama Pearle says, without taking her eyes off me.

Stifling an inappropriate eye roll, I direct my question at Grama Pearle. "I imagine you think I'll be able to discern something from Rye's memories that she's too close to see, something that might be helpful?" She nods. I look at Belamey; his sombre expression remains unchanged. "Rye?"

She sits on the sofa without answering and bows her head forward. Belamey moves away to give us space. As I move and kneel in front of Rye, I bite the inside of my cheeks, mentally tallying how this could go wrong. Being a Memory Keeper gives me the ability to collect and store other people's memories in my mind as if they're my own. I retain them in a state of perfection and can share them with other Memory Keepers if I choose.

"Remember, Kori, it's a skill like breathing," Grama Pearle whispers.

I suck in a deep breath and let it out before I slide my fingers over Rye's closed eyes. Her skin is soft and warm. I can feel a subtle flicker of her eyeballs through her eyelids. Heat grows between us where our skin is in contact. The ashen barrier of Rye's mind is visible, and I push through it until I'm falling through her memories, like Alice falling down the rabbit hole. I'm searching for this one particular memory; this is part of the Memory Keeper process I've given no sort of conscious thought to. I don't know if it is something I do, or something that the other person does, that brings us to the memory that is to be shared between us.

A guttural braying noise comes from overhead. The sky is a vibrant blue, cloudless, but the clouds aren't the only thing visible. Birds are leaving Rye and Cian's condo. One with visible blue feet makes the raucous call again. Because she knows their location is undisclosed, Rye's brain is repeating the words birds, how, and why. Her calm feeling of happiness is shattered, and her ability to draw breath becomes a struggle. Rye's chest tightens. Her dry mouth opens and closes without sound or oxygen. She knows something isn't right.

A brown hawk with a pale streak on its belly and a red tail sails across the sky. Kyson Adelgrief. The other birds leaving the condo blur as the net holding a sharp-shinned hawk, tiny for a hawk, becomes the focus. Cian, in bird form, isn't moving. His blue-grey feathers have splotches of blood on them.

The memory jumps.

The shift is abrupt as self-preservation activates and Rye's appearance changes to a stranger she saw at the market minutes before. Rye quickly dismisses from her mind the option to attack or follow the birds. That action would only get her caught too and the people they care about would never know. Instead, she breaks into a run toward the condo with an irrational thought maybe she saw wrong; maybe Cian is still sleeping in their room.

The door slams into the wall as she throws it open, and she freezes on the threshold. Her illogical thoughts fall away. There's no denying what she saw and is now seeing. The room is in shambles. Furniture is overturned. Mirrors and pictures are knocked from the wall, leaving shattered glass and blood on the floor. There's more blood than seems possible. The air is thick with its stink.

Rye's stomach protests, and she fights against the bile rising in the back of her throat. "Cian," she whispers. "You need help. I need help." She shifts into bird form.

The connection between Rye and me breaks. I stay kneeling in front of her, letting my hands fall from her face. My head drops to rest on her lap. Searching through her memory, I hunt for that clue—the helpful insight she doesn't believe is there. I bolt upright with a gasp, speeding through the internal process of storing Rye's memories in a container in my mind.

"I've got it," I say.

Chapter 3

"The symbol for The Society of the Blood Wind . . . you know, the two horizontal flames flanking swirls? It was in the room, but . . . it was different." I pause, probing inward at the memory. I can feel the weight of everyone's stare. "There were drops added."

"Like tear drops?" Fin asks.

I shake my head. "They were deep red."

Fin's voice is a whisper that gives me shivers. "Blood? The symbol has blood drops added? Sounds like a design Kyson Adelgrief the demented killer would create."

Nodding, I close my eyes. "And there were words in each drop . . . names, our names, and others I didn't recognize. Most of the names I didn't recognize had a line through them." I open my eyes. Working my tongue against the roof of my mouth to moisten it, I choke out my next sentence. "Cian's name was one of the crossed ones." My insides clench.

Rye can't hide the stress in her voice. She's close to shouting when she says, "He *can't* be dead."

"Keep her here," Belamey barks. It isn't clear who is to be doing the keeping, only that *her* is Rye. Belamey's long legs are crossing the room toward the kitchen window Dodo has open. I move slightly so I have an unobstructed sightline. Belamey transforms, and in a blur of feathers, sails out the window as a harpy eagle.

"Blazing hell." I punctuate my cursing with a foot stomp before I relax into the pressure I associate with shifting and take on my hummingbird form.

I speed out of the apartment after Belamey. Because we've had previous conversations over the last few months about it always being worth a flyby, I know he's going to The Society of the Blood Wind house. Every time we check the house—once kept so immaculate—the grass is knee-high, the gardens are overgrown with weeds, and spiders have webs strung across the porch that haven't been broken or cleared away. *How do you make a scary house creepier? Abandonment.*

The distance from Fin's and my apartment to The Society of the Blood Wind house is short. I stumble over the uneven ground when I shift into human form, shocked by the sight. Someone has been here; the smell of fresh-cut grass lingers in the air. Doubtless, that same someone weeded the gardens and displaced the spiderwebs from the front porch.

Belamey and I, both of us in human form, stand on the sidewalk in front of the house. Visible to me is protective magic twining around his body like a glove; I'm wearing a similar body shield. We stand in silence, watching, waiting for movement behind the windows, a motion that hasn't been there in months.

A shadow moves past the downstairs window as I track my eyes over it. It's so fleeting that I'm not sure I saw it. Belamey is radiating tension, but he's frozen in his spot. He didn't observe what I saw, or he'd be trying to attack. I want to get closer, but the sight of the wards set across the property to secure it from unwanted Spellbinder entries keeps me in place. This is as close as I'm getting. I pinch my lips together and strain forward to see the window better. Nothing.

I speak out the side of my mouth, hoping my whisper won't startle Belamey into unnecessary action. "Did you se—"

The house's front door opens, and a slow, lazy creak accompanies it. In response, Belamey's fingers explode away from his palms and from the corner of my eye, I note immobilizing orbs form in his hands. His orbs are laced with pinchers of pain. *Better than death orbs.* Mine are bubble orbs. I like these orbs because whatever is captured inside can't get out; it's a spherical prison cell that I control.

A long-legged bird whose appearance gives the impression that it's wearing capris steps onto the porch. At first sight, I think it's Rye's friend, Archie Meek, known as "Meeks." But this secretary bird is older than Meeks. Plus, Meeks isn't a Society of the Blood Wind supporter. Secretary birds guard specific entrances into the tunnel system running under the town of Lindsay. But they don't guard entrances inside Spellbinder homes; there isn't any need because the family can ward them.

"Ophelia?" Belamey yells. "Ophelia Everett, is that you?"

The bird keeps walking across the porch.

Belamey directs his words to me. "There were stories about Ophelia whispered in The Society of the Blood Wind house. They weren't pleasant. She was captured, held prisoner, and that sort of thing." His eyes focus on the secretary. "Ophelia!"

My muscles are tense, and the hairs on my neck are prickling. "Something isn't right." I hear anxiousness in my voice. I purse my lips and blade my stance so I can release my orbs if needed.

Ophelia—if that's who this is—is still moving toward us. Her lengthy legs make the navigation of stairs bizarre.

Belamey's voice is low, pitched just for me to hear. "Sometimes, growing up, I imagined hearing the word 'help' coming from the walls or under the floors. It was a soft murmur. But if this is Ophelia, I wonder if I was imagin—"

The secretary makes a deep croaking and throws her head back.

"Belamey?" I hiss without taking my eyes off the bird. I sense the threat but can't predict the level of danger. My hope is that Belamey's knowledge of Ophelia will give us the advantage. There's no point in putting her or us at further risk if we can avoid it.

Belamey's orbs vanish from his grip. He launches

himself sideways at me. I don't know how I release my orbs without hitting him. The protective threads of magic that coat his body extend out and around me as we hit the sidewalk. The bird's croaking has changed to a high-pitched tone. Then the bird explodes, not in a mess of guts and feathers, but powder, smoke, and words. It's Kyson's grating voice, repeating two sentences, "Our time will come and with it, each of your deaths. Who's next?"

"Guess we got our message," I breathe, choking and gagging on the mysterious smoke. The odour is complex, a mix of grilled fatty pork, burnt liver, a sweet but musky perfume, and something charcoal-like. "I've never seen magic like this before. Is that what you were expecting to happen?"

Belamey's voice is muffled because his head is turned away from me. "I anticipated weaponization, but not using a living creature. A message designed to hurt more than the messenger is his style, deadly wards, an attack using some of his followers, maybe an exploding inanimate object. This level of dark magic suggests another Spellbinder is teaching Kyson new tricks."

Belamey's weight on top of me is crushing. I can feel rough bits of the sidewalk and sharp pebbles pushing into my back. Before I complain or thank him for saving me from potential harm, his lips brush my ear. "Shift."

The pressure pinning me to the ground eases, and Belamey's wing strokes pepper me with wind before I transform. I follow the three familiar greyish bands that mark his tail feathers all the way to my apartment. We sail into the open apartment window. I note the new wards, amiable for Belamey and me, but not for anybody else trying to enter.

"This day is full of surprises," Belamey growls.

The kitchen is silent except for the rhythmic tick of the clock. Belamey moves his human self to the side, and I notice that Dodo is tied to a chair with the dissipating threads of a magic dome surrounding him. In a few more minutes, the dome will be gone, and Dodo will be able to access his magic and free himself from the chair. His normally sad mouth is set in a tight, thin line, and his dark, watchful eyes are glaring at the second hand on the clock. He won't make eye contact with Belamey or me.

"Should we help him?"

Belamey flicks his eyes in my direction, his semblance grim. "Nope."

My interpretation is that Belamey wants Dodo to learn from the experience. A small lesson while he's safe is better learned than a harder one when the stakes are high. Plus, I think Dodo's predicament is amusing to Belamey.

I scan the room. No sign of forced entry or struggle, so Fin, Grama Pearle, and Rye left by choice, but why? Dodo must've tried to stop them. Understanding of Belamey's amusement hits me. I stifle a snicker; the idea of awkward Dodo trying to thwart three of the most headstrong women I know is too much. My laughter explodes out in a spray of spit and snot, which I try to cover with a fake cough. *Poor Dodo.* I hurry into the living room so my laughter won't wound his pride.

Fin has left Alivia's sketchbook open on the sofa with

a note on top. "Gone to The Fermented Grape to check for the booby." Her printing quivers a bit on the word "booby," a clear sign she was giggling when she wrote it.

Why the rush to find the blue-footed booby?

The very thought of Fin and Grama Pearle together at The Fermented Grape gives me a headache. I knead my temples with my fingers, saying a silent prayer that Rye will keep the two of them in line, safe, and from getting polluted drinking wine. I don't need to question why they would look for a Spellbinder at The Fermented Grape with its history of being a neutral zone—no fighting or settling of old debts allowed there.

Although no living Spellbinder has witnessed a breach in the code of conduct at The Fermented Grape, it's said the building itself responds when someone fails to observe those rules. Since no living Spellbinder can speak firsthand about this, what we know is speculation and dated word of mouth. If Memory Keeper's knowledge of it exists, Grama Pearle and I haven't had access to it.

Understanding how the rules are enforced hasn't been a question. It's just accepted that they are, and judgment is non-negotiable, which makes The Fermented Grape the best place to pick up bits of information and gossip. And if a Spellbinder is going to be found, they're either there in person, or someone will have knowledge about where they are or last were.

I pick up the sketchbook, letting Fin's note fall onto the sofa. The book is a solid weight and carries the fragrance of lavender, and the unique scents of charcoal pencils and acrylic paint. I run my fingers over the page. The paint leaves a raised texture on the paper that's pleasant under my fingertips. Alivia's drawing of the blue-footed booby, from an artistic standpoint, is pleasing to the eye and highly realistic. Even with its comical expression, I feel like the bird is about to leap right out of the page. Its small beady eyes are set too far apart and flank a pale blue bill. Its white, greyish-brown streaked head sits cockeyed on its neck, imploring the viewer to provide it with an explanation for something.

The birds in Alivia's sketchbook are thought to be enemies. They're birds associated with The Society of the Blood Wind, but we thought that of Dodo when we first saw him in the book, and we were mistaken. *What other birds are Alivia and the rest of us wrong about? And how many Spellbinders are linked to The Society of the Blood Wind by coercion?*

Next to the image of the blue-footed booby is Alivia's tidy printing, labelling the bird as Elrod Wigeon, also known as Wimpy. Given that there are no other annotations, Fin, Rye, and Grama Pearle must have gone to The Fermented Grape to find Wimpy, which suggests one of them is familiar with him. But even knowing this, I still have more questions than answers, like why the rush, who knows him, is he a friend or a foe—

A swift surge of air passes through the room, interrupting my string of thoughts. Dodo must have freed himself. I can hear Belamey in the kitchen. "Good job, Dodo. Now tell me, how is it possible?" There's an edge of humour in his tone. "Bested by two old ladies and a normie?" Belamey is shaking with silent laughter.

Dodo's pale skin is crimson when I enter the room. "You've met those women. They're . . . they're . . ."

"Dynamic? Fierce? Formidable?" I offer.

"I was going to say high-powered," Dodo mumbles and ducks his head.

I snort, and Belamey gives a full bark. Dodo raises his head and glares at us. I'm reminded of his age and previous struggles with self-confidence. He's grown so much, but he still has lots to learn. I stop smiling and give Dodo my attention with a neutral expression.

"They're hunting for Wimpy, the booby bird, at The Fermented Grape. I tried to tell them it wasn't safe, and we should wait for you, Belamey, but . . ." Dodo waves his hand around to indicate the predicament we came home to find him in.

"Which of them is familiar with him, Mom or Pearle? And how?" Belamey asks.

"Rye." Dodo shifts his weight back and forth between his feet. "I don't know how, but Rye doesn't believe Wimpy is committed to The Society of the Blood Wind." He grimaces before continuing. "But I don't know why she believes that either, especially given he was there when Cian was . . ." Dodo licks his lips. "Taken."

Belamey nods. It's unclear to me if he is unsurprised by his mother's knowledge and actions or with Dodo not having any answers. I don't waste time questioning him. "Did they identify the other two birds?" I ask Dodo. "Wait. Is Wimpy dangerous, Belamey? Do you know anything about him?"

Belamey shakes his head. "No clue, Kori, which is

why I don't think we should linger here. We need to go find them." What he leaves unspoken is that while the inside of The Fermented Grape is governed by safe zone rules, the outside of the building isn't. Fin, Rye, and Grama Pearle would've been sitting ducks going in and coming out—assuming they made it in unscathed. Even though violence hasn't happened in the vicinity of The Fermented Grape, it doesn't mean it couldn't.

The tone in Belamey's voice has a playful note that draws my attention. "Dodo, try not to get *caught up* in anything else." Smirking, Belamey transforms and sails out the window again, leaving me standing there, nodding in agreement.

I focus back on Dodo, expectantly. Dodo the Spellbinder is also Dodo the bird—flightless. I often forget he can't fly. I continue to look at him questioningly for a second before I remember, and then I roll my eyes at myself.

Dodo shrugs. "I'll stay here. I have a couple more messenger birds to send."

I make a mental note to partner Dodo up with another Spellbinder at the apartment. Even with the wards, we've already pointed out that nobody should be alone. For now, I'm confident he'll stay inside the warded apartment. I pat him on the shoulder, transform, fly out the window, and angle toward The Fermented Grape.

Chapter 4

It's embarrassing—not surprising when I consider how many years I rejected magic—to admit that I've never been inside The Fermented Grape. So, I say nothing when we land outside the unassuming building. I scan around, looking for signs of a threat, but there's nothing. Regardless, I'm thankful that Belamey heads straight in and that he enters before me and can't see my initial reaction to the space. My jaw drops as I take in the greyish penny-tile floors and seven individual bar areas that line the three walls. The bars have marble countertops and nooks behind them, full of wine and fancy glasses. In the middle of the room, there are high-top tables and seating. *If I was a wine drinker . . .*

Given that it's almost dinnertime, I'm surprised that The Fermented Grape isn't busy. Soft instrumental music is playing, but the volume is so low that a couple more groups talking would drown it out. Fin, Grama Pearle, and Rye—even wearing her Astrid persona—are easy to spot. They're in the rear corner at a bar with a man who is out of place in the environment—dressed in dark jeans held up by a spiked belt. He's wearing a black leather jacket over a low-cut ebony-coloured T-shirt.

"Who in the blazing hell is that?" I whisper to Belamey as he cuts through the room.

His shoulders rise and drop. "Must be Wimpy."

I suck a deep breath of air through my nostrils. Belamey stops, and I walk into the back of him. His delicious fragrance—that mix of cardamom, cedar, and lavender, with undertones of cinnamon—fills my nasal passage. *Fiery blazes. His scent is intoxicating.*

He glances at me over his shoulder. "Relax, Firecracker, you're breathing like an angry bull. Try a glass of wine while we find out what's happening with Wimpy." Belamey winks and takes the last few steps to the bar.

Fin, seated in one of the tall chairs, has her feet up on the bar. She appears to have empty hands when I first glimpse her. She's miming drinking from a glass. Given the way she's holding her hand and sipping from it, she thinks she's drinking wine. The memory of Fin the night that Grama Pearle first brought her here— when the Ember stone emerged—pops into my mind. I wasn't at The Fermented Grape with them, but I had been tasked to babysit drunk Fin when they came home. I give silent thanks that she isn't yelling abracadabra while trying to embrace magic she'll never possess.

Fin leans away from the bar. With her chair tipped on the two hind legs, she passes me a glass of red wine. A *real* glass. I flick my eyes to her hand and note the weaves of magic. She's holding a physical glass of wine. Magically concealed, but for what purpose? Fun? Her abracadabra fiasco takes on a new meaning as I realize that she would have drunk from an invisible glass when she was at The Fermented Grape with Grama Pearle. I look at the bartender, and point to Fin's drinking hand.

The bartender winks. "We don't get normies in here very often. So, we have to have a little fun with it."

I smile in response and raise my glass so I can sniff it. Notes of black cherry and chocolate rise from the glass in my hand. Curious, I bring it to my lips. It has a creamy mocha thing going on, which, for wine, surprises me. The room temperature of the liquid turns me off, and I slip the glass onto the bar.

"This is Elrod, but he prefers to be called Wimpy." Fin's eyes are locked on Wimpy's feet. She continues speaking, uncaring if he hears her. "Won't tell us a thing. If Rye doesn't break the no-fighting rule that keeps The Fermented Grape a neutral zone, I'll be shocked."

Grama Pearle has wedged herself between Rye and Wimpy. I can hear him talking, but his voice is subdued, and I can't make out his words. His tone has a calming effect. From this distance, I can see he has tattoos travelling up his neck from under the neckline of his shirt. What surprises me most is that this man, who has to be in his early forties, has blue hair with lengthy grey roots. It's shaved on the sides and long on the top. He has it gelled to the side like porcupine quills.

Watching him interact with Grama Pearle, I note his mannerisms are a well-practised façade to hide his anger and insincerity. Reading people's deceitfulness is a leftover skill from my days as a police officer. As I watch it seems like Wimpy's gaze keeps going distant, like it's glazed over, and he's struggling to stay focused. Belamey has moved into Grama Pearle's place, and she's ushering Rye in the direction of a purple curtain in the corner between our bar and the next one. I assume Rye needs a minute to calm down and that Grama Pearle is trying to create a separation between Rye and Wimpy so that can happen. I know Belamey can ask questions that will elicit helpful information if Wimpy chooses to answer.

Admiring the lavish purple of the curtain, I ask Fin, "What's behind the curtain?" I eye her when she doesn't answer. She's fixated on Wimpy's feet. I roll my eyes and move closer to Belamey and Wimpy. Their conversation is more important than the space behind the curtain. It's a fair assumption that it's the bathroom. Forgetting about it, I listen to the men.

"I like to roam. So, I make my life anywhere and anyway I can, man," Wimpy says, holding his hands open in an apologetic gesture. *Strange comment and accompanying gesture; what did Belamey ask him?* Before I can give thought to what Wimpy means, the front door bangs open, the echo of it ripping through the space.

Wimpy's act of shoving Belamey toward the bar is all that saves Belamey from being hit with the death orb, a surprising act for a member of The Society of the Blood Wind. Does that mean the sketchbook and we, by default, were wrong about another Spellbinder? I detect the foul odour of the death orb before it makes contact with Wimpy. Just like that, he's reduced to sparkling mist that falls in the room like beautiful but unwelcome snow.

My shield is up, protecting Fin, Belamey, and me from whatever might come next. I'm praying it won't be another death orb because I can't block those with this shield. I don't know if anyone can actually block death orbs.

The doorway is dark. The person is standing on the threshold of the doorway, not yet inside the bar. Whoever is there has his features cast in shadow because the light from the street is illuminating his backside. Based on the broad, compact form, I'm guessing it's a man. My ability to see strands of magic shows me he's coated in a magic shield of his own, and he's here to go to war.

I release two powerful sound vibration orbs; my goal is to counteract the effects of gravity for him—his shield won't help with that—long enough for us to meet up with Grama Pearle and Rye behind the purple curtain. My brain hasn't thought beyond that yet.

Fin's knives are moving toward the man in the doorway just behind my orbs. I consider directing a stream of magic at their blades so when they hit him, they'll release a paralytic, but his shield will deflect the knives if I coat them. Two more orbs, Belamey's, are sailing in the same direction. I don't have time to analyze the type because Belamey's hand clamps down on my collar and yanks me backwards as our attacker leaves the doorway to enter the bar. He has a hold of Fin, too. "This isn't the time or place for a battle," he says.

Belamey tugs me and Fin toward the curtain. A merlot-coloured drape of magic—lockdown magic—weaves down the walls of The Fermented Grape. *The Fermented Grape is locking down because its code of conduct was breached.* We dash under the weave before it can trap us. We don't need to be detained for questioning or trapped inside with a Spellbinder who is attacking us. *The lockdown magic probably controls the magic of the Spellbinders temporarily held inside, but it wouldn't control physical combat.* As we tumble through the physical curtain, which is so heavy we have to force our bodies past it, a breeze wafts over us. I blink at the brightness coming through an open fire exit, overwhelming after being in the bar's dim light.

A horn honks. Squinting, I move into the doorway to see Grama Pearle behind the wheel of Fin's '68 Ford Bronco half cab. "Hot dang, this baby has pep."

Rye peeks around Grama Pearle and out the window at us. "We heard the attack. Hustle."

Scanning our surroundings, we're alone. There are no birds, normies, or Spellbinders. It appears our attacker is partnerless. Belamey brushes past me with Fin on his heels. "Come on. If The Fermented Grape's lockdown magic didn't lock that guy inside, we're going to have a hell of a fight on our hands." He vaults into the box of the Bronco with Fin right behind him. I swallow and follow suit.

The parking lot remains empty as the tires squeal with Grama Pearle's overzealous acceleration. The three of us tumble over each other in the box, not bothering to right ourselves for fear we might be flung over the side. I squeeze my eyes shut against the motion sickness caused by her erratic driving.

"Does Grama Pearle have a driver's licence?" Fin yells. I can't stomach answering, so I remain quiet. "I love Grama Pearle," Fin continues, laughing beside me like a lunatic.

Our drive is too short for conversation. The vehicle parks and I hear the doors of the truck open and close. I can't move yet. My nausea can be attributed in part to Grama Pearle's driving and partially to what could have been Belamey's death if it wasn't for Wimpy's sacrifice. I place a hand over my mouth and lie there with my eyes closed.

"Don't be a baby, Kori," Grama Pearle says after the vehicle has been parked for a couple of minutes. "That was some of my best driving."

I lift my hand off my mouth, high enough to speak without muffling my words. "Grama Pearle, I never want to get in a car again if you're driving. I think it's time to consider giving up your driver's licence."

"Oh, I gave that up decades ago."

I can hear feet moving away. The conversation about the brazen attack on us at The Fermented Grape drifts off with them. I continue lying in the Bronco's box.

"Kori, come on," Fin says. I hadn't realized that she was still waiting for me. I hear her step on the bumper, and then the truck starts a subtle bouncing.

"Stop," I mumble, opening my eyes. It's dark out, and the night sky is clear with bright stars. The air is soft and warm. I stare at the stars and take a few calming breaths. "Why were you staring at Wimpy's feet?" I ask Fin to briefly distract myself from Belamey's near-death experience and the rest of that messy situation. I hoist myself out of the truck box. We're in the Just Flavours parking lot.

"Blue-footed boobies poop on their feet."

"Say what?"

"Yeap, they shit on themselves on purpose." Fin shrugs. "I didn't want to get close to his feet, whether he was a Spellbinder or a bird."

I blink at her, but opening and shutting my eyes doesn't convey how painful this conversation is. So, I sum it up with a sentence. "Fin, the walk to the front door of Just Flavours has never felt this long."

"The marabou stork poops on its own legs to cool itself down, and some vultures do too. When we find them . . ." She examines me, contemplating. "When we find the stork and the vulture, both are recluses, nicknamed The Fog and Ruck. I'm not going anywhere near their feet either." Her tone is matter-of-fact.

I pull open the door of Just Flavours and hold it for Fin. She enters. I follow her and turn to close and lock the door. She's prattling on about hygiene and foot poop.

I wait for a break in her speech. "Fin, isn't Griffin a type of vulture?" With a small smirk, I continue walking through the café. My destination is the control room that was built when Fin and Belamey took over Just Flavours. I don't have to look to know that Fin is standing in one spot, opening and closing her mouth. It's a rare moment for me to render my best friend speechless.

I enter the kitchen. The control room is through a concealed door inside the oversized fridge and freezer combo, so I aim for the large doors on the wall to my right. The ridiculous brightness of the space, and the reek of Freon greet me. It doesn't matter how many times I go to the control room, my discomfort at walking into a fridge, knowing that the door is going to close behind me, is almost more than I can handle.

"Kori." Fin is hurrying to catch up to me. I keep moving. "Kori, wait. Griffin can't poop on his feet. I've done things with his feet that—" I hear Fin gagging. I stop walking, wipe the smirk off my face, and wait for her.

She doubles over beside me, dry heaving.

I rub her back with one hand and pull the fridge door closed with the other. "Fin, it's okay. Griffin can't possibly be a bird that poops on himself."

She straightens and stops gagging. I smile with reassurance and steer her toward the control room entrance.

"You're right, he can't be. You've seen the man. He's dreamy."

"Dreamy, yes," I say to appease her. "Griffin is an attractive man, but he's not Belam—" *Shit, did I say that out loud? She'll never let me live down admitting my attraction to Belamey like it's common knowledge.* "Dreamy Spellbinders can't poop on their feet. That's logic, Fin."

"Agreed," she says, but there's a note of mischief in her voice. "Are you finally going to bang Bel—"

"There you are," Grama Pearle says. I face Fin and put one finger over my lips.

The control room has the smell of stale air. We haven't been in here in a few months. We haven't needed our high-tech, windowless surveillance room with fancy equipment and banks of computer monitors. I scan the room. The oversized, comfy chairs are empty. Rye and Belamey are doing something I can't see on one of the computers. "Where's Dodo?"

"Upstairs cooking," Belamey answers without turning. "I called him as soon as my feet hit the pavement. He'll be okay alone in the apartment for a few more minutes." There's nothing in Belamey's tone to suggest he's fazed by having a death orb thrown at him, but that doesn't surprise me.

"We'll just be here a few minutes," Grama Pearle explains. "After speaking with Wimpy, bless his soul, Rye suspects he might not have been acting of his own free will. She asked Belamey if we could access the Allurist Detention Centre computer reports." Grama Pearle winks. "Not exactly legal access, he said, but we can view their records."

I lift my eyebrows at the legality comment but say nothing. In truth, I know how our computer programs work, but I also know what we use them for—Spellbinder crime fighting. So, it's a fair balance in my mind. "Not acting independently? Like when he saved Bel—"

Rye cuts me off, the pitch of her voice sharp. "That would've been his own actions. Despite everything, the Wimpy I knew was a good man."

Rye and Belamey turn away from the computer, cutting off any of my next questions. My pulse quickens watching them. Neither appears comfortable with whatever they've just discovered. I can't decide which of them unsettles me more, Rye with her faraway gaze or Belamey with his intense guise of concentration.

"What the fuck, guys?" Fin says, her voice a mix of concern and curiosity.

Rye peers straight at Grama Pearle. She's wiped any hints of her thoughts or feelings from her mien, and there's nothing discernable in her tone. "Nyoka."

Chapter 5

Grama Pearle and Rye usher us out of the control room and up the narrow enclosed stairs to my apartment with no explanation about what a "nyoka" is. Fin vibrates with curiosity as we open the front door and step into the kitchen.

Belamey is closing the door to the apartment when Fin grabs Grama Pearle by the shoulders. "Tell me," she pleads. "I can't take it. What's a ni-oka? Who was the killer at The Fermented Grape? Was Wimpy's free will altered? By who—" Fin's eyes flare wide, and a visible shiver travels over her whole body. She scrunches her nose up, considering something. "Dr. *Ah-G* Draven would not be responsible for this!" I'm impressed by her dramatic pronunciation of Ague's name and with how Fin sounds both awed and scandalized.

Rye and Grama Pearle are shaking their heads no,

but neither seems in a hurry to explain. I take a second and lift my nose to the air. I cross the kitchen to investigate the source of the rich scent of spices, melting cheese, and something meaty. My tummy gurgles, reminding me we missed dinner. My tastebuds react with a tingle and salivation. "Dodo?" I whisper, closing my eyes and inhaling.

"Turkey and egg skillet, Kori," Dodo answers.

I open my eyes. He has a pile of whole-wheat toast ready. The skillet is a beautiful mess of colours from the ground turkey, egg, Colby cheese, salsa, and avocado. Dodo scoops a heap onto a plate and slides it in my direction on the breakfast bar, pushing the plate of toast after it.

"I've sent messages to let people know there's a threat, and what kind of threat there is." He spoons food onto another plate. "It's up to them to decide what to do with it."

"Good work, Dodo," Belamey says. It's unclear if he's talking about the messenger birds, the food, or both.

Dodo accepts the praise with a dip of his head and finishes preparing plates for everyone. Some people might have made the people he was upset with get their own plates, but that's not Dodo's style. It isn't in his nature to harbour ill will. I know Grama Pearle, Fin, and Rye enough to know that they would have restrained Dodo earlier with tact and apologies.

"Okay, ladies, let's have it now, please," Fin says with a mouthful of food.

I'm nodding, but my focus is on the flavour mix exploding in my mouth. It's a blend of warm deliciousness, and grainy, crunchy toast.

"First, the Spellbinder that attacked us at The Fermented Grape was a man named Alaster Ruckus." Grama Pearle says.

"No way," Belamey challenges, but I note that his usual commitment to what he's saying isn't present. "Ruck is almost ninety years old."

"Eight-six," Grama Pearle announces. I choke on my eggs in surprise, but Grama Pearle just keeps talking. "It was him. I got a peek before Rye and I made it through the curtain. Bear of a man. He looks like the dwarf species the movies enjoy creating. Hard to see him with the way the outside lighting had him backlit. If you could've seen him, he has an always-angry facial expression framed by a bald head, a red moustache, a beard that's highlighted white, and a bulbous nose."

"Okay? But, so what?" I ask.

Rye nods, but Grama Pearle answers. "Ruck is a loner. Stays to himself him, and Caliber Fogarty—"

"You saw the Fog?" I'm surprised by Dodo's out-of-character interruption. He is slack-jawed when I look at him, and goosebumps are peppering the flesh on his arms. My brow draws down, and my brain races, trying to create answers for me.

"Blazing hell, can we please hurry this along?"

Dodo blushes. "Sorry, it's just I've heard stories told about the Fog."

"The Fog is Caliber Fogarty?"

"Yes, he's like an icon for standing up for what he believes in, even if that means standing alone."

"Exactly," Grama Pearle says, taking control of the

conversation. "Ruck is cut from that same cloth. They're independent and solitary. You'd be hard pressed to find an example of them picking a side that wasn't their own."

"To be clear, when they captured Cian, The Fog and Ruck were the vulture and stork, and the blue-footed booby was Wimpy?" I ask.

"Yes," Rye whispers.

I glance at her. My body temperature spikes and I can feel my head shaking back and forth, slow and disbelieving. *How is this woman holding herself together? On the exterior, she's so composed.* I place my empty plate onto the counter and move to Rye—she hasn't picked her plate up, unable to eat if I was to make a guess—and then I slide my arms around her in a hug.

Her arms encircle me. Her voice is in my ear. "Thank you, Kori."

"Maybe, Rye, explain what you heard from Wimpy?" Grama Pearle suggests.

I stand by her side. I feel Belamey's eyes on me, but I can't look at him for fear of what I might recognize in his expression and how that'll affect me. It doesn't seem like an appropriate time to be overcome by desire. My mouth goes dry, and I drop my eyes to the floor, pretending to concentrate solely on what's being said.

"I knew Wimpy from . . ."

I look up to see why Rye has paused.

Her head is tipped, pondering. She brings her head level, nodding with a gentle smile. Her tone is light. "You all know that I live different lives based on the persona

I'm wearing." She alternates from Rye to Astrid to someone I've never seen before and back to Rye again.

"How many people are you?" Fin asks.

"I can impersonate anybody, Fin, but I've *lived* as many people over the years, with Astrid being one of my main disguises. Some of my favourites were Lark Rey, a magical artifact collector, Eira Sage, a security detail for safe house clients, Citrine Rose, a justice seeker, and Miss Avery, a nanny for Belamey, Kyson, and Kieran." Her eyes stray to Belamey, who closes his and gives a subtle nod. *Not fresh news to him based on his reaction; the rest of us have varying degrees of surprise on our faces.*

"No more question about any of that now, Fin. Let's just say I knew Wimpy from one of my other lives. He was a drifter who made his life wherever he chose and however he could, often in lawless ways. But he always preferred being alone, which is why his recent string of behaviour makes me almost certain that something or someone else was driving his actions."

That drifter stuff sounds familiar. Wimpy said almost the same thing to Belamey when we were at The Fermented Grape.

Rye sighs. "Wimpy wasn't a Spellbinder who had a lot of friends. I don't know that I would consider us friends . . . acquaintances maybe? Either way, I knew him well enough that today, I sensed he was scared because his own actions confused him. It wasn't that he wouldn't tell us what happened, but more that he couldn't, which made me wonder if maybe he was being controlled."

The change between Wimpy's focus and unfocused gaze!

The room is silent. Fin, Dodo, and I gaze at everyone, trying to put together what we've just been told. Fin swats at the air like she's hitting invisible obstacles. Her voice is sharp. "No, no, no. That's not enough of an explanation."

Belamey chuckles. I feel a moment of feverishness and fight the urge to fan myself. *This is getting ridiculous.* Thankfully, nobody is paying attention to me.

"Well, Fin," Belamey says. "Based on Mother's hunch about Wimpy, we were checking the records from the Allurist Detention Centre on our computer system to see if there've been any disturbances there. Besides Ague, who you already pointed out is on our side, there's one other person with the kind of magical strength and skill to manipulate and control Spellbinders. Nyoka Cifarelli."

Dodo, Fin, and I share an ah-ha moment. Grama Pearle already new what Belamey and Rye were doing on the computer and why.

The Allurist Detention Centre is a Spellbinder prison hidden in the mountains deep in northern Canada. Each jail cell controls the magical strengths of the prisoner held in it. When inmates are out of their cells, they're fitted with ankle cuffs that inhibit the use of magic, including the ability to shrink and shapeshift. It's a scary place housing nefarious Spellbinders.

"Let me guess," Fin says with excitement. "She's no longer a resident of the Allurist Detention Centre?"

Belamey puts one finger on his nose and uses the pointer finger on his other hand to point at Fin. "Bingo," he says.

Fin does a happy dance. "Why and when did she get released?" she asks. "And where can we find her?"

"They didn't release her, Fin," Rye corrects.

"She was broken out of Allurist Detention Centre?" Dodo and I say in unison. We stare at each other, our faces mirroring astonishment. "How?"

Belamey is moving to clean up the mess from our meal. "Either she broke herself out or someone else helped her escape. Reports on file weren't complete. So, either they don't know or are unsure how to write it up. Either way, Nyoka was returned to her cell to wait for her lunch and gone when her lunch showed up."

I'm tapping my foot and feel a headache coming on. *This is taking too long.* My next words sound harsh in my ears. "The how of it doesn't matter right now. The why seems to be connected to Kyson and his revenge. But how does any of this help Cian?"

A smash, followed by the vibration of shattered glass hitting the floor, makes us jump. We spin toward the noise, each of us armed to protect ourselves. The apartment is warded, which offers a measure of protection against ambush, but something just happened. Silence settles. There's no attack and no more commotion.

Belamey stalks into the living room. We follow. The window is broken and an unfamiliar urn, the kind that holds human remains, is lying in the debris. *Cian? Please don't let this urn have human remains inside.*

Rye's legs give way, and the crunch of her knees smashing the floor is followed by a cry of anguish that I never thought I'd hear this amazing woman make.

"It can't be," Fin whispers, her eyes pleading.

My head is shaking a frantic no, but my shoulders are shrugging. I've no idea and no control. None of us do. Belamey is on the ground holding Rye, who's trembling with silent tears. Dodo is standing over them, see-sawing his weight between his feet.

Grama Pearle flicks all her fingers, targeting the glass; a weave of magic that reminds me of the hollow outline of puzzle pieces sweeps over the broken glass. It catches each shard, fitting them together, and moves the repaired window pane into place. She moves toward the urn with purposeful steps.

"Grama Pearle?" I'm trying to ignore the sinking feeling in my chest.

"There's only one way to know if . . ." Grama Pearle can't bring herself to say Cian's name. She steels her spine and clears her throat before speaking again. "There is only one way to determine if these are human remains and whose they might be, Kori." She twists open the urn and reaches inside.

I watch, dumbfounded, as she pulls out a fistful of ashes and releases them into the air. Her other hand is clutching the onyx and glass cremation necklace that holds some of Grandpa Ian's ashes. The strange green-grey glow of his ashes is a regular part of Grama Pearle's outfit; he's always with her. I saw her toss some of his ashes in the air once before. Instead of scattering, the ashes pulled together to form a ghost of Grandpa

Ian's snowy owl. He protected us that day. One of Grama Pearle's other unique abilities is to call the bird of a deceased Spellbinder into non-permanent manifestation using their ashes. She's a Ghoster.

Rye's head is buried in Belamey's shoulder, so she's unaware of what Grama Pearle is doing.

My chest is tight, and my brain is screaming for time to hurry as I watch Grama Pearle release the unknown ashes into the air. I lick my lips and narrow my vision to the ashes.

I can hear Fin repeating the same words, "Don't be a hawk; don't be a sharp-shinned hawk."

The scattered ashes pull together. The raptor that takes shape from the ashes is slender but big. Its large, brown-black wings contrast against its white body. It closes its wings, almost six feet when open, and stands in the living room, eyeing Grama Pearle. I'm squinting at its black, strong-hooked beak, trying to decide what is coating it.

"Is that blood?" My tone is soft.

I'm not sure if I hear Grama Pearle correctly when she mumbles, "Lipstick."

"Osprey." Fin breathes. "It's not Cian."

Grama Pearle's eyes are wet, and her voice breaks. "No, it's Ague."

Chapter 6

The coffeemaker's gurgling draws me from sleep. My body feels warm and relaxed. I'm on my back, cuddled between two pillows, and I feel rested in a way I didn't expect after yesterday's experience.

I lay unmoving with my eyes closed, pondering why I feel so good. *Someone is breathing in my ear.* I crack my eyes open. Out of the corner of my left eye, I observe the back of the sofa, so I'm not in bed nestled between pillows after all. I look down and note a man's arm draped across me. *Belamey?* There's a lightness in my chest, and I have the urge to giggle. That's right. Rye and Grama Pearle slept in my bed. I slept on the sofa, and Belamey *was* on the floor.

A motion to the right catches my attention. I turn my head enough to see Belamey beside me with his eyes closed and Fin, in profile, standing behind him. She's pumping her whole body like she's humping the air. If I wasn't worried about waking Belamey, I would beat Fin with the pillow under my head. She stops her action and focuses on me, raising her eyebrows in question. When I just stare at her, she pumps her hips twice.

"Fin, I can assure you—like you and Griffin—when Kori and I have sex, there'll be no need for you to ask. Anybody inside this apartment will hear our groans," Belamey croaks, his voice coming awake with him. My ears turn red and my stomach flutters. "Morning, Firecracker," he says to me, rolling off the sofa.

Fin fans herself and sighs. "You two need to get to it. I won't even ask to watch." She pauses like she's reconsidering. After a couple of seconds, she lifts her right shoulder up and down, cocking her head toward it, and smiles. "I won't ask that, but I do want to hear all the dirty details after." She smacks Belamey on his ass and strolls into the kitchen. Belamey chuckles and shakes his head.

He yawns, stretching his arms into the air and arching his back. His coal-coloured T-shirt pulls up, revealing a toned stomach. His black cargo pants hang loose on his hips, and it doesn't appear he's wearing boxers. My mouth is open, I'm panting, and there's heat in places that aren't typically that warm. *Think about something else, something not sexy. Blazing hell, don't use the word sex.*

"There's coffee," Fin calls to us.

"Coffee, Firecracker," Belamey says, looking down at me on the sofa. "Let's get us some." He reaches down and helps me up.

"Coffee would be good," I say. *Coffee, coffee, coffee. Not sex. Coffee.*

Grama Pearle and Rye are seated at the breakfast bar when we enter the kitchen. Grama Pearle's eyes are puffy from crying. Last night, Rye and Grama Pearle spent a few hours telling us entertaining and surprisingly sweet stories about Ague, whom Grama Pearle lovingly referred to as a "psychological nightmare." Grief about Ague mixes with mild relief about Cian and hangs in the air like a cloud.

Fin smirks at Belamey and me and thrusts coffees at us. Dodo blushes and passes us both a fancy glass filled with repeating layers of granola, yogourt, and fresh fruit. "Thank you, Dodo. This looks yummy," I say.

Belamey doesn't drift far from me, and I don't mind. I inhale a deep whiff of my coffee, steal a sip of the hot brew, and sit it on the counter. Nobody is eager to talk. I dip my head down and watch my spoon as I push it through the yogourt and berries, feeling the slight resistance change to smooth gliding in the yogourt. The berries' sweetness, the granola's crunch, and the yogourt's creaminess are a perfect blend. My mouth enjoys the juxtaposition of velvet and crunch.

As I eat, I mull over the little I learned about Nyoka last night. Because of Ague's unexpected death, Rye and Grama Pearle directed their focus on her, causing the bulk of the information about Nyoka to be connected or in contrast to Ague. Nyoka was Ague's mentor. But where Ague wanted people to believe she was crazy—her way of keeping people at a distance and protecting herself—Nyoka has a legal diagnosis that labels her psychotic. Her known disorders include dissociative identity, antisocial personality, and histrionic personality, which are characterized by impulsivity, disregard for rules and norms, aggression, manipulation, emotional instability, and no remorse. Locked in the Allurist Detention Centre for the past three decades for crimes Ague testified about, it's easy to assume that Nyoka's ability to connect with reality vanished.

Another interesting tidbit was that The Society of the Blood Wind attempted to recruit Ague, but she couldn't be swayed to support their beliefs or methods. She wouldn't align with them. Ague's ethics and method of conduct were questionable, yet she had the general good of everyone she worked with in mind.

Nyoka tried to join the ranks of The Society of the Blood Wind, but Dolion and Nekane refused her. There aren't any lines that she won't cross. She's said to feel no pain but loves inflicting it—a fact that makes me think of Kyson and his deceased twin, Kieran. Nyoka craves power; control, for her, is a drug.

The very thought that there's a Spellbinder so evil that The Society of the Blood Wind won't accept her is terrifying. Because Nyoka isn't sloppy or careless, some Spellbinders believe The Society of the Blood Wind had a hand in Nyoka's capture and the availability of evidence against her. Some believe The Society of the Blood Wind acted as an "anonymous" party, supplying tips about Nyoka's whereabouts and planting material objects at her crime scenes to make her guilt indisputable.

If there are other Spellbinders who are masters of mind control and manipulation, like Nyoka and Ague, they're keeping it a secret. Some Spellbinders try to learn, but surface learning versus an innate ability are two different things.

I'm struggling with Grama Pearle's descriptions of Nyoka's brutal crimes when I pit those against the description of Nyoka as an old witch with natural beauty and a permanent grin. My mind wanders to the crone of folklore—a sinister crone whose evil is visible in her appearance, as if it seeps out of her. I know that this may still be the case. She likely exudes a wickedness that a person's intuition would sense, but I'm wrestling with what my mind wants to visualize and what I'm being told.

The clicking of the lock on the apartment door draws me from my musings. The only person with a key is Griffin. With all the wards in place, I don't have concerns that someone is using magic to open the lock. Fin must've come to the same conclusion because she's a blur moving past me. The door opens, and she's off the ground. How Griffin catches her and keeps the pair of them from tumbling down the stairs behind them is an act of magic, even if real magic isn't involved.

Griffin's throaty laugh fills the room. "Hello, Finley." His low, rough voice oozes confidence.

We wait and watch with patience while Fin and Griffin share a long and dramatic hello. Their display increases my desire to do something similar—but naughtier—with Belamey. *It's not the time for our first lusty moment. Are my body and mind sabotaging my sexual cravings by yearning at inopportune times? Nonsense: grief and comfort go together.* Belamey, clearing his throat, interrupts my inner argument. Griffin reluctantly sets Fin down on her feet.

"You're early, aren't you?" Belamey asks. "What was your mission?"

Fin is standing before Griffin, smoothing her clothing and brushing her hair with her fingers. Griffin steps aside so he can address the room without distraction. Attractive and sure of himself, his feet are spread, with one hand resting in the pocket of his jeans and the other arm hanging at his side. He starts with the words nobody wants to hear. "We have a problem."

"No shit," Fin says. From my place in the room, I see every head turn to look at her. Fin shrugs. "What? We have a huge problem. We know that."

Refocused on Griffin, I watch him study her before taking a slow gander at each of us. He nods. "It seems we have more than one problem then." His previously gentle smile becomes a grimace. "Cian."

At the mention of Cian's name, the energy in the room becomes more tense, and Griffin pauses, having felt the change. His almost clear blue eyes narrow. "The quick version of my mission is that when Travon Coyer, the warden for the Allurist Detention Centre, was found murdered, Cian asked me to investigate what he felt was a series of missing Spellbinders who were turning up dead."

Travon Coyer, why is that name fresh in my mind? "Griffin," I interrupt. "Could you tell me a couple of other names of the missing or deceased, please?"

Everyone is looking at me. I close my eyes and focus on Griffin's voice. "Sarin Thornhart, Coppin Boleyn, Essie Bradbury, Ra—"

My eyes pop open. "Those are all names that were crossed off in the blood drops from Rye's memory."

Collective gasps greet my announcement. Griffin surveys us before he speaks. "Someone can fill me in on what that means next. But most of these dead or now presumed dead Spellbinders had connections to the Ember family, the creation of Spellbinder laws, and the Allurist Detention Centre. The Allurist Detention Centre has a lot of new staff being trained. The shit with the Allurist Detention Centre, like missing staff and strange accidents, has been going on for a while, but until recently, it was happening in a way that wasn't drawing any attention."

I'm blinking like an idiot. "Nyoka." I try to swallow, but my mouth has gone dry. My tongue feels leaden and pasty. "This was part of the plan to get her out. It can't be her organizing this from inside the prison. That means she has someone outside the prison, loyal to her, who is having the staff killed and replaced with specifically picked Spellbinders. It seems like an extreme way to break out just one Spellbinder. Do you thi—"

"Do you think they'll bust out more dangerous Spellbinders?" Fin cuts in, taking the words out of my mouth. The thought is too much to put into words, and I'm thankful that Fin put it out to the room so I didn't have to. I lift my coffee and swish a mouthful of the liquid.

"Nyoka Cifarelli?" The level of concern in Griffin's voice is high.

"Yeah," Belamey says with a huff of angry air.

"Does Ague know?"

Fin is beside Griffin in a few steps. Her arms slip around his waist. She lowers her head and places a tender kiss on the side of his neck. Griffin is frozen. My eyes go wide. I feel panic because I've never seen him display anything other than cool, calm, and confidence.

Grama Pearle and Rye have lowered their heads. Dodo is statue-like; I almost forgot he was standing there by the stove. Belamey is shaking his head. "I'm sorry, Grif. Ague is dead."

I cringe. Belamey's direct sentence and use of the word "dead" is how I was trained at the police academy to deliver the news to the loved ones of the deceased, so there's no misconception or false hope. But it's always felt harsh to me, especially here in a room full of friends so close we're family. My breakfast has turned to an unpleasant lump in my stomach that no amount of coffee will melt. My eyes stray to the coffee pot and back to Griffin and Fin.

Griffin says nothing. His face moves through a series of frowns, grimaces, and scrunches. "Excuse me," he manages, then exits toward his and Fin's bedroom.

It's general knowledge that Griffin and Ague had a work history together, but I suspect, despite the fifteen-plus-year age gap, they might have more carnal knowledge of each other. They were never touchy-feely, and Ague's respect for personal space was non-existent, but that ignorance of personal space just felt different between them. It was charged with an intimate energy. If anyone else noticed, they didn't say, and it wasn't something that I felt I should discuss with Fin. If Griffin and Ague had sexual knowledge of one another, it was before Fin entered Griffin's gravity field.

"I'll fill him in on everything," Fin says, hurrying after him. "When he's ready," she adds. She closes the bedroom door. Soft music plays in their bedroom, and I know she has turned it on to afford a measure of privacy.

Chapter 7

I move to the coffeemaker. It's going to be the kind of day where caffeine fuels and sustains me. I wave the coffee pot at everyone in the room, asking if there are more takers, and top up the willing. I sit the pot down and lift my mug to my lips. Eyes closed, I draw a deep inhale of the steam. It's warm and fragrant. My first sip smarts my tongue, but it doesn't stop me from taking another.

I blow out a sigh. "Okay, we've learned nothing useful from Griffin, and knowing that Nyoka is roaming the world doesn't help us, either. We assume that Nyoka and Kyson are connected, and that connection is related to Cian being abducted. Now what? We need to move. Too much time has passed already, in my once-professional opinion." Moments when I miss my life as a police officer are rare, but in situations like this,

I'd love access to the resources that being a cop provides.

Rye and Belamey speak at the same time. "We have to get inside The Society of the Blood Wind house." They stare at each other, nodding.

"There has to be something there that we could use to find them," Rye says. "Kyson's resources are limited. Rumours are that even Society followers don't want to be led by him, and some are refusing outright. He's killing the vocal resisters to scare others in to following him. Dolion and Nekane were bad, but Kyson . . ." Her voice trails off.

There's no need to say more. Kyson was raised to kill, and nobody is outside his kill zone. If he takes a fancy to kill someone, they're dead. *Cian.*

I hadn't heard Fin's bedroom door open; it isn't like her to be quiet. So, I jump when she speaks. "Nope, no way. I'm not going in those tunnels, and I refuse to let anybody else go. The last time we were in there, those starving, sightless murk salamanders hunted us. There were bats in eternal sleep, waiting to be woken so they could feed on us. Let's not forget the beautiful, deadly sparkles and who knows what else is down there."

At Fin's mention of the tunnels, my eyes stray to Rye's hand. The faerie ring, half responsible for saving Rye's life when we were in the tunnels before, is snug on her finger. Its silver spiral is a tree adorned with beautiful green leaves. I've never seen another ring like it.

I'm surprised to hear a small laugh escape from Rye. "No, Fin, we aren't going in the tunnels. We're going in the front door."

Rye places a key on the breakfast bar.

My mouth drops, so I move my hand up to hide my surprise behind the mug of coffee. I'm not liking this plan, whether we enter through the tunnels or the front door. I understand the need for action, but this seems like suicide. We could walk into a trap. "Belamey, you remember when we were there yesterday, and the secretary bird blew itself up to . . . to, what? I don't know, scare us, hurt us, give us a message? That was just on the sidewalk in front of the house. What's going to happen *inside* the house, if we can even get in? There are all the wards protecting the house."

Before Belamey can respond, Fin is talking again. "You think a key from . . ." she trails off and frowns at Belamey. "How old are you again?"

He shrugs, unwilling to play along.

"You think a key from thirty-some-odd years ago is going to open the front door to The Society of the Blood Wind house?" Fin cocks her head and stares at Rye.

Rye's eyes are fixed on the key. "I don't think. I know."

Fin moves her gaze to the key. It's an average key, not unique. She leans forward to have a closer inspection. Her nose scrunches up, and she pokes at the key like it might electrocute her. When nothing happens, she leaves one finger lingering on it. "No way, I don't buy it." A slow smile builds, and she dances her eyebrows. "But I'm in; let's try."

"Seriously?" I huff. I look at Grama Pearle and Griffin to see if they object.

Grama Pearle shrugs. "It isn't like we have a lot of options."

"I understand that, but . . ." I trail off, not sure what else to introduce as an argument. Accepting defeat regarding this decision, my voice is toneless. "And the wards, how will we navigate those?"

Rye slides the key out from under Fin's finger. "It'll work, Fin, because why would they need to change the locks? Nobody is brave or stupid enough to enter that house uninvited." Rye lifts her eyes to me. "As for the wards, Kori, we have you. If you can describe the threads, then Pearle and I should be able to deactivate those wards. Any wards we can't turn off, we'll trip."

Rye's love for Cian is driving her; the first time she's allowed herself to love openly and without fear since she went into hiding, and now, she might lose him forever. I emit a long, low sigh. There are some magics most Spellbinders can perform, but those are specific to family lines and individual Spellbinders. Being able to see threads of magic is a unique magic. We don't know another Spellbinder, beyond me, that can do it. I down the rest of my coffee.

I notice Griffin hasn't rejoined us. We are going to need everyone with us, but only if they can function to make safe decisions. "Is Griffin okay?"

Fin nods without making eye contact with anyone. "As good as can be expected. He'll be out in a minute."

I trust Fin's assessment of Griffin's state of mind and an hour later, the seven of us are in front of The Society of the Blood Wind house. Our plan is simple: be vigilant, deactivate the wards, enter the house, check for any clue that might help us, and get back out as fast as we can. If we get separated, we're supposed to just get out.

We're standing on the sidewalk in the same spot Belamey and I were when Ophelia Everett became another of Kyson's—and likely Nyoka's—victims. The sun is beating down on us, and there isn't a hint of a breeze. Beads of sweat are forming on my forehead and trickling down.

"There are three individual wards." My voice is strained. I have a fleeting wish that I had an iced coffee to moisten my dry mouth. "They're all semi-permeable. So, certain Spellbinders can pass, but given the pattern of these weaves, I wouldn't recommend we test if we're one of them."

Grama Pearle is scowling at the house like she's trying to visualize the strands I disclosed. "Describe one for us, please, Kori."

I push the fluttery feeling in my chest away and nod curtly. My voice is steady. "A green and brown mesh covers the ground. It comes out about six feet from the house." I glance at Grama Pearle.

She considers, her eyes scanning the ground. "Is it static, or does it have movement?"

"There's a very subtle ripple at ground level. No part of this weave rises off the ground."

Rye and Grama Pearle exchange a look.

"Could you please fill us in on what you're thinking?" Fin's hands are on her hips, and her head is moving between the ground, Rye, and Grama Pearle.

Grama Pearle sticks her tongue out at Fin. Satisfied

with her childishness, Grama Pearle smirks. "The weave is over an area of ground that's infected with quietus mites. Normal mites feed on decaying matter in the soil, but quietus mites feed on living matter. The weave Kori sees is keeping them contained and will hold the weight of any Spellbinder that's welcome in the house. Anyone who isn't welcome . . ." Grama Pearle opens and closes her mouth without finishing her sentence. She turns to Rye. "I can cast a carpeting spell to get us over. I'll need a few minutes to get it in place. Can you find out what the next ward is?"

Rye nods and turns to me.

Sighing, I strain my eyes because when I first saw this weave, I thought perhaps I had a migraine coming on. The air has blurry splotches like retinal auras. They come and go in different spots all around the yard. Rye calls them gale dust. The wind energy trapped in those blurs is enough to kill on impact—blow a body apart. She weaves a bubble orb and, with my direction, catches one blur inside. I give her a complete description of the weave associated with the blur captured inside the orb, and she begins disarming it, hoping it'll disarm the whole ward.

"The last ward is a fire ward," I tell them with certainty. "It's a yellow, green, and bluish twine with movement. The way it moves causes the colours to bowl over one another, creating a rolling flame. It's encircling the house."

"Can you throw a water orb on it so we can get on with this? It's creepy just lingering in front of this house and waiting for who knows what." Fin says.

I consider her suggestion, but it just seems like that would be too easy. "Somehow, I don't think that's a good idea."

"Nope," Belamey says. "Fire magic, at least fire wards, is designed to have a more powerful response to someone trying to douse it with water."

Fin turns to Griffin. "Can we use one of those fun body shields to pass through?" She sounds a bit too eager about the shield idea. When Griffin chuckles, I'm certain they've used the shield during one of their sexual romps. "I suppose that means no," Fin says with a pout. "So, how do we get through the last ward?"

Dodo surprises us when he spins his hands in a circle, creating sparks as his hands move faster. When he stops, there's a fire ward encircling him.

I can't keep my mouth from falling open. "When did you learn to do that?"

Dodo blushes. "It worked? You can see my fire ward?"

I nod and take a fast look at Grama Pearle and then Rye. They're still working on dismantling the other wards. I missed hearing Dodo's question. "Pardon?"

"Does it look like the one moving around the house?"

"Similar. Your fire is yellow. The one warding the house . . ." I watch it, studying it. "The one warding the house is almost blue."

Biting his lip, he hesitates.

"Dude, you got this," Fin says. He gapes at her, and she winks. He turns a deeper shade of red but lifts his chin and pushes out his chest.

A fizzing noise circles the house. "I neutralized the

gale dust," Rye announces.

"Dodo?" I say with my head tipped to the side.

"Well, fire wards have a weakness." He peeks at Belamey. "Can you suck the oxygen away from my ward?"

"Can't see it," Belamey says, eyeing me.

I point to the level of Dodo's body where the ward is so Belamey has an idea of where to aim his magic. Belamey creates a weave of icy blue, and I watch, wide-eyed, as he draws the oxygen from Dodo's ward into the icy blue funnel. It's like the funnel breathes it in, dispelling nothing.

"Keep doing what you're doing, but walk into me," Dodo tells Belamey. "You shouldn't burn because there should be a space where you are pulling the oxygen from my ward."

I can see that it's safe for Belamey to walk through.

"Shouldn't?" Belamey says. Dodo smirks and blushes. Belamey walks through Dodo's ward unharmed. Dodo drops the ward, and Belamey smacks him on the back. "Good work."

Fin points at the house and waves her arms. "Um, Kori said the ward on the house is blue."

"You need to take more oxygen from it. It needs to be done with haste, and our crossing will need to be speedy." Dodo crosses his arms and steps away, showing that's all he has for us.

"Carpet is ready," Grama Pearle says.

"Let's get sucking," Fin says, slapping a hand over her mouth to smother a laugh.

We form a plan and line up in a single file with

Grama Pearle in the lead, followed by Griffin, me, Dodo, Fin, and Rye. Belamey brings up the rear. I copy Belamey's weave for the icy blue funnel. Everyone, except for Fin, formulates a similar weave.

We start across the carpet Grama Pearle laid over the quietus mites. Everyone's stride is uneven, and it's like we're performing a drunken group shuffle. The carpet squishes under my feet, and there's a hum of energy as the weight of my steps excites the mites. My skin crawls with apprehension.

I pinch the inside of my cheeks between my teeth. Holding my cheeks in forces me to draw breath through my nose, and I'm working to keep my inhalations and exhalations even. One thing I learned as a police officer was that controlled breathing helps manage fear and tunnel vision. It also prevents panic and improves decision-making in high-stress situations. Grama Pearle turns when she reaches the porch so she can keep her suction on the fire ward. The rest of the Spellbinders in our group do the same until Belamey steps onto the porch.

The porch feels stifling. A trick of my overactive imagination. The fire ward doesn't give off heat, at least not until it sets someone on fire. The increase in heat is my internal response to the anxiety building in me.

"It sure is a relief that the wards only work in one direction because if we needed to get out fast, we'd be screwed. And not in a good way," Fin says, her voice too bubbly for her dark point.

I shoot her a glare, which she ignores. Her eyes are locked on Rye's hand, which holds the key to the lock on the front door. There's the expected rumble noise of the key sliding into the lock.

Rye turns her hand to the right, and the lock tumbles open. Rye doesn't hesitate. With her left hand positioned on the doorknob, she flings the door open. It protests with a creak but swings inward.

We give a collective sigh of relief at the dark emptiness that greets us and step inside.

Chapter 8

I've never been inside The Society of the Blood Wind house. The first thing I notice is a mellow fragrance that is sweet and vanilla-ish. It feels out of place with my expectations for this space. We've crowded in through the entranceway and are standing in one of the two formal living rooms. The ten-foot ceilings make the space feel airy. The focal point in the room is the curved staircase.

"Yum, is that marshmallow?" Fin's head is on a swivel.

Belamey snaps his fingers, and the fireplace sparks to life.

"Haven't you had enough fire activity for one day?" I ask with a grimace. Turning to frown at Belamey, a flush creeps across my cheeks and my stomach drops. I move to his side. "Are you okay?"

He nods, but says nothing and doesn't look at me. *He's not okay.*

In my curiosity and shock over being inside this house, I didn't give any consideration to Belamey returning to his childhood home for the first time in years. My eyes flare wide, and I whip my head in Rye's direction. *If this is hard on Belamey, how difficult is it for Rye?* There's no evidence on her face or in her mannerisms to give me a clue what she's feeling. She's a master at schooling herself. *Check in with Rye later, at a more appropriate time.*

A shuffling gait descending the stairs draws our attention. Although it doesn't sound like a threat, I know better than to be fooled by assumptions. My body shield is on, and I summon orbs in my palms. My group has likewise taken defensive action. An elderly man with weathered skin and rheumy eyes stops on the bottom step, leaning on an umbrella, its knife tip wedged into the wooden stair. He glowers at us.

I'm blinking more than necessary at what I'm seeing. The man has a grey ponytail, a goatee that's made full because of excessive nose hairs merging into it, and tufts of hair poking straight out of his ears. His appearance is made more bizarre because of the ripped and patched loose jeans that are rolled to show his ankles, topped with a blue plaid suit coat, dress shirt, and stripped cream and navy tie. He isn't accessing any magic, but I'm the sole person who can see that.

"Caliber Fogarty," Grama Pearle says, "imagine finding you here."

His mouth moves like he's going to respond to

Grama Pearle, but snaps shut before he can. His body twitches.

"He's trying to fight it." Fin, positioned on my right, sounds awed. "Someone is controlling him, and he's resisting. Or trying to." Her voice is low, so only myself and Griffin—standing on Fin's other side—can hear. I know Fin is reading the disjointed way the Fog is moving. She's relating it to her own experience a few years ago, when Ague used Fin to demonstrate the little effort she needed to gain control of someone and hold it.

The rasp of the Fog's umbrella knife being pulled from the wood draws my awareness to the stairs in time to view threads of magic weave up and down the umbrella as he bangs it down. The smell in the air changes to a familiar one that has a sweet-spicy and cream scent. It's warm and woodsy while exotic.

"Cian!" Rye is intimately familiar with the smell; it's his fragrance. Her voice is a rush of air, like a sigh and pleading jumbled together.

The Fog lifts his umbrella and bangs it again. A velvet bag, rounded by whatever fills it, appears in the Fog's right palm, which he has held out in front of him like he's making an offering. His voice is nasal. "Cian put up a good fight. Noble to the end but—"

A throwing knife lodges into the Fog's throat before he even finishes the sentence. There's a glowing magic heating the blade. I swear the Fog mouths the words "thank you" as his rheumy eye releases a teardrop. His knees crumple as though in slow motion.

My head snaps toward Fin because she's the person

in our group who I know is armed, on a regular basis, with knives. But it's Rye I see closing the distance. In her right hand is a translucent cinnamon-coloured orb. There's no mistaking the frenzied electric pulse inside of it, a glowing shade of white. Nobody in our group moves to stop her. I can assume that everyone is as stunned as me by Rye's impulsivity and out-of-character choice.

Why kill the Fog? Cian is dead, which is what brought us here in the first place. The Fog is being controlled, so he continues to pose an unknown threat and one we won't be able to get any information from because of the manipulation he's under. We have no idea what a Spellbinder is capable of while under someone else's influence. Rye had to come to those conclusions faster than me. But, couldn't the Fog have provided some clue about who is the puppeteer? So, many thoughts are speeding through my mind as I watch Rye.

The death orb in her hand is undersized, more like a large marble than a tennis ball. She's coated the same hand in an ivory weave, making it appear like she's wearing a magic glove.

"You're free!" she yells, slamming the orb into the centre of the Fog's forehead. His body is reduced to a thick cloud of shimmering mist that releases an audible sigh. Rye is kneeling with the velvet bag of Cian's remains cradled against her chest. She's turned her face up, expressionless, as tears spill from her eyes.

"Hello, Rye," a voice cracks with pubescent hormones.

Rye levels her head, glaring up the stairs at a teenage boy. "Hello, Blake."

I'm discomforted by their casual greeting, the way they're behaving like today is an ordinary day. How long the teen was waiting on the stairs, watching, isn't clear. He's about halfway up, standing with his chest puffed out. He's trying to appear tough as he leers at the scene with big, steel-blue eyes. I note his shaved head. His baldness mimics his mentor, Kyson.

"Everyone," Blake says with a dramatic hand gesture, "your noble Recruiter, Cian, is dead. Kyson wanted to say a few words about Cian's demise, but as you can see, Kyson isn't here. He knew you'd come, but he couldn't wait. Regardless, he's glad you all made an appearance." Blake transforms into his crow. Wings flapping, he steers toward the upper floor of the house.

The room drops into a darkness so thick—magically enhanced—that I can't see Fin, who was a foot away from me a second ago. Voices ring out in the darkness, amid the chaotic din of struggle. There are dim flashes of light trying to cut through the blackness, but whatever this is it won't allow light to glow.

My breathing is loud and uneven as I flail my hands in front of me, scared to use defensive magic for fear of who I might injure. My swipes find emptiness time after time. I keep my shields up, hoping they'll be sufficient against this attack. I'm calling out, but the abnormal absence of light smothers my words.

Just get out. My brain screams the words of the plan. *If we get separated, or if the situation becomes one where we can't help each other just get out.* My jaw aches from holding my teeth together, and my chest feels so tight that oxygen is restricted.

I drop into a crouch, using instinct alone. I shuffle through the blackout, staying low. *You've been in similar situations in your cop life, Kori. Remember the assault suspect in that one house's basement? You went down—foolish—alone. Flashlight out in front, you moved toward the breathing, and then your flashlight died. You lived through that; you'll live through this, too.*

What feels like a door handle rams into the front of my shoulder, and pain lances down my arm. Grunting, I stand, tracing my hand over the door's face and follow it forward. As I step over the threshold onto the porch, the blast of natural light is painful. I turn to the open doorway. It's an opaque wall of darkness.

Fin comes charging out, running into me with her shoulder. The force knocks me sideways, but I keep my footing. She doesn't stop. She thunders straight across the porch, down the stairs, and skids to a halt on the far side of her warded Bronco. Her hair is almost as wild as her eyes as she scans for any other escapees.

Grama Pearle hurries past without seeing me. Her run is a mix of shuffles and hops. "Start the truck," she calls out to Fin.

Shoving his mother in front of him, Belamey comes out next. Rye's clutching the velvet bag.

"Move, Kori!" Belamey hollers at me.

I cast a glance at the doorway before I follow Belamey. He's stuffing Rye into the truck and pushing in beside her as I hop into the truck box. The summer air is stifling, a reminder of the oppressive darkness we escaped. I shiver despite the heat. *That was too close.* Fin has the truck idling, and we're all watching the door.

Griffin flies out of the house on lengthy, narrow wings. As a black-bearded vulture, he lands in the Bronco's box and shifts. He bangs his hand on the roof of the cab. "Go!"

The truck rockets forward, and Griffin lowers himself into the box with Grama Pearle and me. I grab Griffin's arm, "Dodo?"

Griffin shakes his head, his expression grim. I cover my mouth with my hand and stare at the house as we drive off. A familiar, broad body steps outside. He takes a wide stance and holds his hands in fists. The long, braided beard and moustache that Grama Pearle described are unmistakable—it's Alaster Ruckus. The last I observe is of him turning and going inside. *Who else was moving around in that blinding darkness? And why is nobody chasing us?*

Belamey ushers Rye inside when we get to the apartment. He doesn't pay any attention to the rest of us, trusting we can navigate ourselves into the building. I watch Fin as she climbs out of the truck. Her forehead is crimson with welts.

She shrugs. "Ran into the wall twice, trying to get out the door." She marches off after Grama Pearle, who is cutting a fast pace toward the stairs up to the apartment. Griffin and I share a look.

"No Dodo?" I ask, hoping his answer will have changed from the first time I asked.

Griffin shakes his head and walks away. I follow. The

sickening feeling in my stomach is almost enough to overwhelm me. *Guess I know why nobody chased us. They already had what they wanted—one of us.*

Belamey eyes each of us as we come in. Rye is beside him, statue-like. She's closed down any emotion, her go-to survival technique. I close the door, and he keeps watching it, waiting for the seventh member of our group to enter. He was so focused on Rye that he didn't notice we had three people in the truck box, not four. Griffin claps his hand on Belamey's shoulder and locks eyes with him. "I tried, but I couldn't get to him."

The silence that follows is so heavy that the gurgling of the coffeemaker makes each of us jump. How Fin got the coffee pot brewing so fast, I don't know, and I couldn't care less because I need a coffee really bad. Nobody has said anything about Cian, but the grief-stricken faces I see speak more than words.

"Cian trained us for the possibility that we might lose him." My tongue feels heavy as I speak, and I'm blinking back tears. "He would tell us to fight now and mourn later." Grama Pearle casts her eyes down and waits. Fin, Griffin, and Belamey are nodding, but none of us move or say anything more.

Fin's voice is unusually muted when she breaks the silence. "I hate to be the one pointing this out, but Kyson holds us responsible for his twin and his mentor's deaths." She takes a minute to grimace. "Rye and Belamey were part of The Society of the Blood Wind family at one point, making them priority targets."

"But he didn't take them, Fin," I point out.

She raises her eyebrows. "I know. He took people

who were important to them first. By killing someone they hold dear, just like we did to him with Kieran and Dolion, he causes them pain. Remember what Kyson said? He said, 'I promised that our time would come, and with it, each of your deaths.' He plans to kill us all," she says with an indifference that makes me shake my head, "but Rye and Belamey will die with the grief of loss filling them."

She holds her hand up. "I know what you're thinking, Kori. He didn't take you to hurt Belamey. He took Dodo. But think about it; he wants to hurt you too."

Fin and I both stare at Grama Pearle. "I wager he'll come for Grama Pearle next to hurt you, Kori. If I was a psycho killer, I'd save your murder for last because if you and the Ember stone had never come along, then none of this would have played out the way it did."

The room is silent again. Fin's assessment holds a lot of weight. My eye is twitching. The rest of the muscles in my body are quivering, and I'm gulping air while my emotions ride the waves of fear and anger. My voice is shaky when I respond to Fin's comment about Kyson hurting me. "If he's trying to hurt me, he could take anybody in this room and have that effect. If he's trying to hurt any of us, that also holds true."

We're eyeing one another—a voiceless assessment of what we all mean to each other. I close my eyes, push my fingertips into my temples, and move them in tiny circles. "I get it. He'll crave hurting all of us, so he has us linked by pairs so his devastation can have maximum impact. I've seen similar things during my career as a cop. Think of a spurned lover who tries to get revenge on the person who rejected them by threatening or attacking that person's family and friends. Those acts isolate the person who did the rejecting and cause them pain and humiliation. It's extra suffering before the direct assault on the rejector.

"If I put myself in Kyson's place," I say with a shiver of disgust, "I'd pair Grama Pearle and me together. Griffin and Fin make a pair. After separating these two groups, he'll come around again." I swallow, trying not to gag on the sour taste in my mouth. A chill travels over me. "Rye and Belamey, or it could be Griffin and Belamey. Either way, it leaves Belamey and then me."

Chapter 9

Rye relives something only she can see. Her expression becomes pained and her eyes clouded. For Rye to show emotion, especially for longer than a glimpse, is unnerving. She stopped responding to our questions and allowed Belamey to lead her to my room so she could try to sleep.

It's early afternoon. Belamey is pacing the kitchen like a caged cougar. His hands ball and his arm muscles flex, then relax, flex, then relax. "Coward." His husky voice is deeper than normal, a growl, as he talks to himself. "Hiding behind other Spellbinders and having Nyoka control them to do his dirty work."

We know he's talking about Kyson. Fin's head is bobbing along in agreement. Griffin is quiet, his eyes tracking Belamey's back-and-forth prowl. Grama Pearle is pacing as well, but hers is a thoughtful shuffle.

My anger is a mix of panic, sympathy, and impatience. I'm hot, my pulse is speeding, there's an ache in my throat, and I have a mild headache. *This is nothing compared to what I'm sure Rye and Belamey are feeling.* My brain speeds through scenarios.

"We're thinking about this wrong," I spit out.

Belamey casts his eyes at me but keeps pacing. Griffin and Fin focus on me.

Grama Pearle stops and points. "You're right, Kori. We are thinking about this the wrong way." She gives a solo nod.

I scratch the side of my head and push out a breath of air before I start speaking. "Would Nyoka have a place they could hole up, a command centre of sorts, even though she's been imprisoned for so long?" Belamey freezes and turns toward me. I raise my shoulder and my expression slides into a questioning countenance.

"Hot damn, Kori," Grama Pearle says.

Belamey closes the space between us and kisses my forehead. My stomach flutters. I don't trust myself to utter words for fear he might hear a tremble in my voice. I realize that I'm holding my breath; my tongue darts out, and I lick my lips.

"Kiss her on the lips," Fin blurts out.

Belamey doesn't skip a beat. "Not now, Fin. It isn't the time."

My heart feels like it's shrinking. I stifle my disappointment about Belamey's comment about it not being the time. *What? Did you just acknowledge that you want Belamey to kiss you? Kori, this is getting old, I tell myself.* "So, hideouts?" I ask the room.

"Like a cave or a hole? Nyoka gives the impression of a villain that would like a dark, damp space to hide," Fin adds.

"Two possibilities," Grama Pearle and Belamey say in unison. They look at each other, surprised by their paired response.

"Neither is a cave or hole, Fin." Belamey waves his hand, giving Grama Pearle the floor. Fin sticks her tongue out at Belamey, but he isn't focused on her.

"Well, three actually, but one isn't local, and given the plans they're executing, they won't be in another country." Grama Pearle scrunches her face, considering, and shakes her head. "Nyoka and Kyson would both want to be close to enjoy making their marionettes do their spin and spring."

The left side of Grama Pearle's mouth pulls up and her nose is pinched on one side. "You won't like this, but Nyoka loves the tunnels. She haunted the area under the normie super jail all those years ago."

"Blazing hell!" Fin thunders. Our drawn expressions, including Griffin's, don't phase her. "What? It's a fun way to curse."

"That doesn't seem like a great or convenient place to hide," I offer the room, my eyes still cut to Fin.

"No," Belamey agrees. "But it's well protected and not a spot that someone would think to search first."

"Fair. What's the other place, though, Grama Pearle?" I ask.

"The old Victoria County jail."

"The 1863 jail? Isn't it haunted?" Fin whispers. "Do

you know how many people they publicly hung there? Rumour is they tried to convert it into a museum but . . . but shit kept happening. The dead walk! That doesn't sound any better than the tunnels." She sucks air rapidly so she can continue before anybody else tries to speak. She's louder and more eager now. "That jail has housed some of Canada's worst criminals like P—"

"Fin, do not start listing off prisoners," I bark.

She pouts, and her voice comes out without enthusiasm. "Let's scope the 1863 jail out first. You all know how I feel about the tunnels. Plus, it's closer."

"Somebody needs to stay with Rye," I say, scanning Grama Pearle and then Fin. "We're just going to surveil so we can make a plan and gather resources." I make eye contact with Belamey. "We're observing, right?"

He eyes me and nods. "Grif?"

Griffin stands and stretches. He leans over and kisses Fin before she can launch an argument about staying put. I don't linger to see anything further. I push the window up, transform, and fly out, trusting both men will be right behind me.

The old jail is around the corner and up the road. I land, and transform, staying in a crouch in the bushes across the street, admiring the Romanesque Revival style of the building. The air is still, not a hint of a breeze. Belamey and Griffin land, shift, and huddle beside me. There's no movement, but I didn't expect there would be.

"Threads of magic aren't visible, so it isn't warded, at least on the exterior."

"They're here, or they have been." Griffin changes

positions. "Scan the ground. There are too many feathers, like there's been birds struggling."

We fall silent, considering what that might imply. Minutes pass, but nothing changes; the jail's yard remains empty of life forms. There are no incongruous sounds. Restless energy is oozing out of me, and I'm rocking on the balls of my feet from my crouched position. Even though I know our planning and thinking equals safety, my brain keeps cycling through two thoughts: we have to hurry up and do something, and this is taking too long. Beside me, Belamey is fidgeting with his eyes glued to the jail. His impatience is visible in the tightness of his eyes and the roll of his shoulders.

Griffin clamps a hand down on Belamey's shoulder. "That's all we need to know. Let's get the troops." Belamey's head nods with the slightest of hesitation, his eyes remaining hyper-focused on the jail. Satisfied that Belamey will follow, Griffin transforms and flies toward the apartment.

I rock on my crouched legs and rub my arms, trying to brush away the feeling of misfortune. *Oh, man. This won't go well.* "We can't figh—"

But Belamey is up and moving. His fast, determined steps increase in speed until he's running toward an iron gate recessed in the wall.

I push my legs hard, trying to catch up to him. My brain switches into police mode—I'm going to do my job, and I'm coming out again. My senses heighten without the use of magic.

Belamey yanks the gate open, which I now realize

wasn't clicked closed. *How'd he notice that from the other side of the street?* I rush in after him. He pauses inside to allow his eyes to adjust to the dim light. I breathe in the smell of decay and neglect. It feels like it's pushing down on me with the weight of untold stories, loneliness, and despair. It's such a powerful feeling that my throat thickens with the pressure of mounting tears. My voice is monotone. "Do you feel it?"

"Yeah."

A wet pop, like a water balloon being smashed onto the floor, echoes in the space—an orb popping. The sound corresponds to light, white and blinding, filling the hallway. My blinking is frantic against the brightness, cursing that we're trapped in a hallway with no cover or concealment. My shield was coating my body before I even entered the jail's yard, but now I've dropped into a defensive crouch. Spinning toward the footsteps approaching the gate behind me, I trust Belamey to face whatever is in front of us.

"Hello cousin." Kyson's grating voice is like nails on a chalkboard.

Belamey tenses and stands.

I stand too, keeping us back-to-back so I can watch the gate. Whoever else is out there hasn't made themselves known yet. I suspect it might be Ruck or Blake, since they seem to be Kyson's trusted henchmen.

Behind me, Belamey's voice is a snarl. "Where is Dodo?"

"Oh cousin, what is it with you and that *Dodo*? You threw away your life with The Society of the Blood Wind to hide that boy from Nekane, your father, and Dolion. You robbed Dodo of a life of greatness."

"Where is he?"

"He's safe enough," Kyson exhales, "for the moment. He's with Nyoka. What a charmingly crazy Spellbinder she is. What do you think of her, Ruck?" Kyson's laughter fills the space.

So, Ruck is with Kyson. I fight the urge to turn and look. Why address a question to Ruck in the middle of an argument with Belamey? It seems absurd in the middle of everything that's going on, but I'm thankful because it has told me three things. First, Kyson isn't facing Belamey alone; Ruck is with him. Second, we're outnumbered, and third, it isn't Ruck that's lurking outside. Maybe it's Blake.

I can't shake the uncomfortable feeling that there's a hidden message in the strange question Kyson asked Ruck. *Is Nyoka controlling Ruck? Does Ruck like Nyoka's power? Or is it something else entirely?*

Belamey charges, magic forgotten. I can't see them, but I don't doubt the bloodlust working to consume them both. They have built up a lifetime of hatred between them. The power of it heats the space. I fight the desire to turn, sensing that whoever is outside the door is waiting to catch me unaware.

"Kyson, you coward!" Belamey hollers.

Kyson responds with laughter that fades—he's fleeing.

Belamey's next words are strained, a note of fear in them. "Ruck, fight it, man."

Belamey is pushing against me, moving backwards,

slow and steady. "Move out, Kori, but no sudden movements," he hisses. "Ruck appears like he's delaying. He's either waiting for Kyson's command to attack, or maybe he's fighting Nyoka's spell. I can't tell."

I turn my head a bit and cast my eyes the rest of the way. The threads of magic coming off Belamey are vibrant. He has a wall of protective magic blocking the hallway between us and Ruck. Movement draws my attention back to the gate. I don't wait. I launch an orb of air mingled with a paralytic and follow it with a dissipating dome to capture whoever is there and restrict their movement. No point in taking any other chances. A grunt tells me that my dome hit somebody.

A force hits me from behind and launches me out of the gate with Belamey. Ruck must have thrown some kind of orb at us that rebounded off Belamey's shield and threw us backward. We bang and bump into each other as we hit the ground, rolling into a tangle.

Belamey and I both throw orbs at the gate as we scramble to our feet. Belamey angles himself like he plans to race inside. My skin is tingling a warning, and my heartbeat is pounding in my ears. I grab Belamey and scream in his face, my eyes drifting between his face and the gate. I shake him to get him to focus on me. "We have to leave."

His eyes cut to the gate. Thunderous footsteps echo from inside. "We can't fight Ruck ourselves," I continue, "especially a Ruck controlled by another Spellbinder. We don't know Nyoka's capabilities. He could have heightened strength and heightened pain tolerance."

Belamey glances at Blake, the Spellbinder trapped

under my dissipating dome, and bars his teeth. Belamey shifts.

I consider Blake for a second. A dark stripe of peach fuzz coats the upper lip of his scowling mouth; he can't be more than thirteen. There is so much anger and loneliness in his eyes that my heart hurts for him. Wincing because there isn't anything I can do to help him, I transform. Belamey and I fly toward the apartment. They didn't follow the last time. Hopefully, they won't this time either.

I'm not sure why Belamey lands at the bottom of the stairs and doesn't go back in through the window we'd used when we left. Perhaps the emotions he's struggling with have distracted him. Either way, he shifts and tramps up the stairs with me on his heels in human form.

The box at the top of the stairs stops us cold.

"No magic clinging to it," I say automatically.

Belamey bends and lifts the top off without picking it up. The apartment door opens, likely in response to the thump of Belamey's feet. Belamey makes a noise I've never heard him make before.

Griffin, standing at the open door, is quick with his response. His air hands grab Belamey and keep him from tumbling down the stairs and taking me with him.

Grama Pearle is beside Griffin in a second, and a stream of calming magic shoots into Belamey. She has a force behind it that scares me; Belamey loses consciousness. Griffin's magic air hands carry Belamey inside. I peer at Grama Pearle, who is staring down into the open box.

I gaze down and gag.

The box is full of ashes. On the top of the pile are two dull red feet with yellow claws. The feet of a dodo bird.

Chapter 10

We leave Belamey on the sofa, unconscious. Grama Pearle's calming magic will continue working on him, so when he wakes, he'll be in control of his emotions and able to experience a level of grief, anger, and whatever other feelings he needs to without them crippling him. He also won't be inclined to act impulsively.

My eyes feel raw from how hard I rubbed them, trying to scrub away the sight of Dodo's feet. My breaths are shaky, and tears well in my eyes. I step away from Belamey on the sofa. I need space. I need to process. Swaying slightly, I turn to leave the room. I plant my feet wide and remind myself we have work to do. My jaw sets in determination, and with a fast stride, I exit the room.

Back in the kitchen with a coffee gripped between my

hands, I explain what happened after Griffin flew away. "We have to deal with Kyson," my voice is steely. "And Nyoka. I'm past the point of caring if it's just or legal punishment."

"Kori, who was the Spellbinder you left under the dome?" Fin asks with her head cocked to the side.

"Blake." I scan my brief memory of our encounter. "Based on the strings of his magic, his magic was average. He wasn't able to resist or break the dissipating dome, and he didn't make any over-the-top attacks on us. So, in my opinion, he wasn't being manipulated by Nyoka. He was acting on his own choices," I say, shaking my head and fighting my mounting frustration.

"I received a messenger bird advising that more prisoners are missing from the Allurist Detention Centre," Rye says, coming out of the bedroom and interrupting Fin. Rye exudes tranquility and focus, one of her many skills and what we've grown to expect from her. "More lifers. So, the worst of the worst."

Fin pours a mug of coffee. "So, they're still recruiting out of the Allurist Detention Centre. Isn't there something we can do about that?"

Grabbing onto Fin's question about stopping the prison breach makes us seem like we're avoiding thoughts of Cian and conversation about Dodo's death. We are equally desperate for action that will keep us distracted and feeling like we are righting this horrible situation.

Griffin nods at Grama Pearle like they're acknowledging a need to talk about something. Their shared look puts me on edge; it's dark and uncomfortable. Grama Pearle's tone is serious but respectful. "It should be me, Griffin, for all the reasons we can leave unspoken. Don't dishonour our relationship by arguing with me."

Griffin bows and holds the position. "Thank you, Pearle."

Grama Pearle lays a hand on his arm, and he stands.

"Smoke and ashes," I huff at them, unable to hide my confusion with what feels like a coded conversation that I lack the information to decrypt. "Why are you acting as if someone is agreeing to go to their death?" My eyes flick between them, my scalp prickling with an unease I can't yet identify.

"I know the emergency protocols to lock the detention centre down. There are a few of us who do, and it would appear a number of them were the Spellbinders who went missing and turned up dead. I'll leave right now and make sure it's locked down." It doesn't seem like Grama Pearle is talking to me, but I realize this is important information if I want to understand what's going on.

Lockdown? Spellbinders being killed because of this knowledge? I'm working through these new details, but not swiftly enough.

"It isn't safe to go alone, Pearle." Rye's physical appearance moves through several people, and when she stops, she has assumed the persona of Astrid. "I think this skill set might help get you inside the prison. Plus, then you won't be travelling solo."

Anticipating Grama Pearle's objection, she puts her

palms up toward Pearle. "I won't stay. Once I know you've entered the prison, I'll leave. Whatever comes after for you on the inside will be yours to deal with. Independently. And I'll find someone from that area to travel back with me and join our forces here."

My gaze darts between Grama Pearle, Rye, and Griffin, and my head is shaking no as understanding settles over me. *Grama Pearle plans to travel to the Allurist Detention Centre on a mission without us.*

"Deal," Grama Pearle says.

No deal, my brain screams, but I can't force the words past my tongue.

We watch Rye move into the living room and bend toward the still-sleeping Belamey. Trying to release the tension I'm holding, I roll my shoulders as I stare at them.

Rye whispers something in Belamey's ear, kisses his forehead, and returns to us. Hefting her chin at me, she says, "You should tell her, Pearle." Rye shrugs. "Just in case."

My stomach drops, and the tension in my shoulders climbs up my neck. "I don't like the insinuations of that sentence. I don't like the implications of anything spoken in the last few minutes." My impatience makes my voice sharp.

"Kori, I need to share a memory with you. No time to argue. You won't like it, but I don't care. I don't enjoy having to give it to you. But, should something happen to me, there needs to be someone to take over the lockdown responsibility. We don't know if all the others who have this knowledge are dead or if some have just gone into hiding. I can't risk this information disappearing with me."

"That doesn't help the feeling of dread that's building in me, Grama Pearle." I sigh, but don't argue. Her tone, coupled with our current situation, won't allow it. I move close to her and sniff the air. A skunk stink is faint but present. "Um, why do you smell like marijuana?"

She flicks her hand at me. "Thought I'd try something new." Her face pinches. "But yuck! Pot is not my thing. I'll stick with my wine, thank you very much."

I hear Fin snicker and home in on it. "Fin, we'll talk after."

"What? I didn't give it to her. I prefer wine, too."

Grama Pearle is flicking her hand again. "I didn't get it from anybody in this apartment, Kori. I hit up that," she pauses and tips her head to the side, "that . . . homeboy? Is that the right term? I don't think it is. Anyway, I watched him sell to a few other individuals one day when I had nothing better to do, and then I got him to sell to me." She takes on an offended expression. "He thought it was funny."

So many questions run through my mind—and lectures, too—but I just shake my head. Grama Pearle will never change. I lift my hands to her closed eyes. The connection between us is fast, and I don't notice the feel of her flesh or struggle through any mental barrier. What she wants to show me is instant in my mind's eye.

The Allurist Detention Centre is shrouded in a heavy fog. It's a wide stone castle built into the side of the mountain. Its tiny recessed windows give it a slight prison feel, but it's because they're a claustrophobic size. A deep archway is the only entrance in sight.

The vision moves, the viewer is walking, and I'm seeing through that person's eyes. It doesn't feel like Grama Pearle; this person's height and movement are different. The viewer walks slightly bent forward with slumped shoulders. Grama Pearle's outgoing nature and confidence are missing. I see puffs of mists when air is expelled by this person's breath.

The archway is a deep tunnel that leads to a gated entrance. Earth dwellers are coming and going via the door and a stone access portal in the ground inside the tunnel. They're identifiable by their fog-grey and unnaturally smooth skin, enormous noses, short stature, and strange clothing.

The entrance to the prison is a square-shaped, two-storey brick room with lights suspended from the second-floor ceiling. Jail cells are visible on the second floor. The viewer turns, opens a heavy steel door, and continues walking. The pace is steady and unhurried, as if they are trying not to draw unwanted scrutiny from inmates or staff.

Eventually, the populated sections lead to quiet, empty areas. The hallways narrow and an orb light is required because there are no lights or windows this deep in the prison. A modest round door marks the tunnel ending. The viewer's hands make a sequence of magical gestures—a hand spell—a click echoes in the hallway, and the door opens. Inside is a stone computer. There isn't any other word for it. A series of stone buttons are pushed, and a lever is pulled.

A rumble, like the earth itself is speaking, responds to the stone computer. The rumble becomes a shake, and the viewer is running, pushing the limits of their speed, back the way they came. The shake becomes a full quake. Through the populated areas, the viewer keeps running, apparently the singular person who understands what's happening. Regardless, there's a chaos of voices trying to figure out what is going on.

The viewer slides into the entrance space, feet scrambling for footing.

Outside the door, the viewer loses footing and hits the ground hard, tumbling. The front entrance of the Allurist Detention Centre appears. It's sinking down and backward into the rocky mountain. The viewer can't stand in the tunnel; the ceiling is too low. A crouching run ensues. The end of the tunnel is visible.

I can't feel the viewer's emotions, but I'm aware of my growing panic watching the exit continue to decrease in size—the space compressing.

The viewer makes a dive attempt.

The rough stone of the ground scratches and jabs. Hands grab the viewer's wrist and pull, but it's too late. The tunnel's opening sinks out of sight, crushing the viewer's legs off at the hips.

The vision ends. I feel disorientated, so I leave my eyes closed. One of my hands covers my mouth and then drifts to my breastbone. My other hand is still on Grama Pearle's head. As much as I don't want to, I'm remembering the last few seconds of the vision, given that the whole thing is in my head now. It's real, but unreal.

Grama Pearle and I open our eyes and stare at each other. The glossy redness of her eyes reminds me that my grandmother dipped a toe in the drug pool. She pats the side of my head. "She shouldn't have tried to get out. The prison and the earth dwellers put rules in place for a reason."

I control the urge to roll my eyes at Grama Pearle's statement about rules. "That was you who tried to pull her free?"

Grama Pearle shakes her head. "No, it was your great-great-grandmother. She was a Memory Keeper, too."

My mouth is dry. "Okay. And who was the Spellbinder that died?"

Grama Pearle's smile is tired. "An old friend of the family. That's all that's important."

"And this is what you plan to do? How will you get out?"

"Escape? No, I plan to stay locked down and accept my fate, whatever that may be. I've lived a good life, Kori."

I can't speak. The thought of never seeing Grama Pearle again isn't something I can put words, thoughts, or emotions to. I'm blinking and standing with my mouth gaped open.

"Don't make it sound hopeless, Pearle," Rye says. "You can't predict the future any more than the rest of us can."

I gape at her, close my mouth, and scrunch my brow.

She pays no heed to me. "The prison can be brought to the surface once we've neutralized the threat. And *we will* neutralize Kyson and Nyoka."

Wordless, I turn my head toward Grama Pearle, expecting her rebuttal.

"I haven't spoken to an earth dweller in years." Grama Pearle's voice is wistful. She rubs her palms together. "Who is to say what they may or may not do? Only they can bring the Allurist Detention Centre back to the surface. The decision will be theirs."

Rye is hugging Fin and Griffin as she talks. "We need to go, Pearle. It's a long flight that far into northern Canada."

Grama Pearle's arms lock around me in a crushing hug. I return the squeeze. My fear is a rock in my stomach. We break apart, and we both have moist eyes, but refuse to cry. Neither of us has words for each other. Grama Pearle moves to Fin and hugs her, whispering something. I think I hear Grama Pearle tell Fin to keep it secret until the time is right, but I'm unsure. She slips something into Fin's hand. Fin, for once, is speechless as she slides the object into her pants pocket.

Grama Pearle gives Griffin a brief hug, then she shrinks to four inches as Rye transforms into an indigo bunting. I'm thankful that Grama Pearle's bird is flightless. The hoatzin, aptly named a stink bird, would gas us out of our small apartment. Rye stays low on the floor so Grama Pearle can climb on. Then they're up and out the window. A whistling tune of "sweet-sweet-chew" comes back to us. A pretty song from a pretty bird, but sorrowful in the present situation.

Fin, Griffin, and I are alone in the kitchen, staring at

the open window.

"Finding Nyoka and Kyson requires a plan. It would be good to have one by the time Belamey wakes up," Fin says. "He's not going to like that we just let his mother go off on what has the potential to be a suicide mission."

I close my eyes, tip my head up, and take some cleansing breaths. *Please let them both return to us safely.*

Chapter 11

Belamey wakes a few hours after Grama Pearle and Rye leave. His face is a mask of grief and sorrow. Finding out that Rye left and what she's planning to do doesn't help him much. But with the aid of Grama Pearle's calming magic saturating his system, Belamey isn't volatile or wanting to race out impulsively to do who knows what to the objects of his wrath. He's thinking as he drinks an evening coffee.

"We'll have a celebration of life for Dodo, Cian, and Ague once it can be the focus of our attention. We owe it to them to finish our mission and then honour their lives with no distractions," I say, my heart clenching. Nobody objects.

My brain is rolling through everything that's happened. I rub my temples. "Fin, what did Grama Pearle give you before she left?"

Fin squirms in her seat before she peeks at me. "She said that great imagination will be required from me before this is through." She sputters for a second, gives a strangled laugh, and clears her throat. "It's a secret."

Noting her discomfort with my asking, I decide to leave this mystery alone—at least for now. I can assume that whatever Grama Pearle gave Fin, it's infused with magic. Griffin and Belamey either aren't curious or they register Fin's unease and don't ask questions.

Silence lingers for a beat before Fin breaks it. "Do you think they're in the tunnels?" No need to clarify which "they" she's talking about—Kyson and Nyoka.

I push harder on my temples, rolling the flesh in mini circles, considering. "I don't, but I suspect they want us to think they are."

"Why?"

"Trap. If our theory about Kyson's order of snatching us is correct, it'll need to be a place that's disorientating and has dangers of its own." I frown. "He has to assume we're at least suspicious of his plan."

Fin is tapping her fingernail against her teeth. She stops and clicks her tongue. "So, you're thinking they're in the old jail?"

I peek at Belamey to determine if he's on the same page. He's staring into his cup like the answer might be in there. "Belamey, you want to weigh in on this?"

He looks up. "Kori, you make a good point about Kyson's assumption, which is why I think they *are* in the tunnels. If I were him, I'd take two of us prisoner at once this time. As you pointed out, Kyson will want us suspicious of his plan to grab *one* of us. Us focused on the tunnel's hazards, keeps us from thinking he might change his plan of attack."

Fin lets out a whistle and smacks her hand down on the breakfast bar. "Hot damn, that's brilliant. A double play because the net is tightening."

"Griff?" Belamey says.

Griffin nods in agreement.

The feeling of icy fingers creeping up my back makes me shiver. Fin's voice is quiet. "I don't want to do that, guys. The tunnels are not a place I want to be." She's rubbing her palms up and down the legs of her pants. "I will," she says, "but I don't want to."

"Nobody is going to make you, Fin. It wouldn't be a bad idea to have someone above ground who can sound the alarm if we don't come out." With an alert gaze and a set jaw, there's no hesitation in Belamey's statement. He's gone from grief to resoluteness—but his anger lingers.

"Not tonight, though, right?" I ask, uncertain. "We need at least one or two other Spellbinders with us."

"Dodo," Belamey's voice breaks on his name. "Dodo's messages provided a warning and a call for assistance. But the call for help said to protect family and loved ones first." Belamey surveys the room and the open window. His meaning isn't lost.

"We're alone! You think we have to do this alone?" Fin's voice drips with scandalization. "Nope, no way. I don't believe it."

I'm staring at the window like I can will an ally to fly in. The day has turned into a dark night. The racket of nightlife drifts up to us: laughter, voices, traffic, and horns. As I stand there, staring and paying no mind to the conversation going on around me, I realize the kitchen feels different tonight without Dodo. The tantalizing smells of his cooking, the sizzling, crackling, bubbling, chopping, and whisking are all absent. There's a hole in our routine, in our circle of friends, in our life, that'll never feel the same. My eyes feel watery. I close them to avoid the blurred vision from tears and swipe my sleeve under my nose, which has started to run.

Sorry.

I focus on the solid feel of the floor under my feet, the hum of conversation, and the rise and fall of my chest as I draw and expel air. When I have my emotions under control, I open my eyes to return to the conversation and almost jump out of my skin. Sitting on the windowsill is a lanky owl whose feathers are a mottled brown-orange. The bird has a surprised expression that's comical when paired with extended ear tufts that point straight up. It hops from the sill and transforms before it hits the floor. The young woman standing before me has a sassy air of self-satisfaction. She runs a hand over her hot pink hair, changing its colour to a purple so dark it gives the impression it's black.

"Brynlee?"

Brynlee's emerald eyes fix me with a challenging glare. "Cousin."

My mouth drops open and I roll my eyes to the sky. She rolls her eyes back at me and scans, giving a chin raise in greeting to Griffin, Belamey, and Fin.

"Can you do that trick to my hair," Fin asks, racing by me and hugging Brynlee like they're long-lost friends.

"Sorry, Fin, I can't. But I do have a friend that can dye it for you the normie way."

"Darn," Fin says and thumps her feet before returning to her place at the breakfast bar. "I just had to be born a normie, didn't I?"

Ignoring Fin, I wave Brynlee into the room. "What are you doing here?"

She shrugs. "Well, our family has grouped at your mom and dad's place. They're following Dodo's warning and staying indoors and together, which is what they wanted me to do. So, I wanted to do the opposite. I thought you guys might need an extra Spellbinder to help rescue Cian." She catches the energy swing at the mention of his name. "Oh." Brynlee's surveying, taking stock of who is and isn't in the room. She knows our usual group and the fact that Grama Pearle was here with Rye. Her manner hardens.

"Grama Pearle and Rye have gone to the Allurist Detention Centre to activate emergency protocol. So, to the best of our knowledge, they're safe." I lick my lips and steal a peek at Belamey out of the corner of my eye. It's hard to swallow. "Dodo is . . ." I blow air out of my nose.

"Sorry," Brynlee says.

I remember Brynlee's relationship with Ague and blanch. "Ague, too," I say, dipping my head.

Brynlee gasps. She lifts her hand and snaps her fingers, igniting a tiny flame, extinguishing it, and then repeating. It's her way of calming herself, not dissimilar to my use of air currents and chakra stones.

Brynlee is just like her mother, my aunt Rune, so I know there isn't any point in trying to deter her from helping—plus, we need extra people to stand with us, and I'm certain where Brynlee's loyalty lies. I open my mouth to fill her in on the rest, but she stops me with a headshake and turns to watch the window. We all glance that way as well.

"Are we waiting for something or someone?" I ask.

"You bet," Brynlee says.

A crow swoops in through the window, shifting. I'm staring at a girl who is younger than Brynlee. Brynlee is in her early twenties—I'm a decade older than her—which makes this girl a mere teenager of fifteen or sixteen at the most. Fin gasps. If Griffin reacts to our guest, it's a silent reaction.

Belamey finds his manners before the rest of us. "Hello, Mayhem."

Mayhem's mouth pulls into a straight line before relaxing into a neutral guise.

"Um," I give Mayhem a half-hearted smile and nod of greeting before I narrow my eyes at Brynlee. The last time I had heard anything about Mayhem was from Belamey. He had called her a rogue who didn't know where her loyalties were.

Brynlee straightens her spine. "Give me some credit, Kori. I pick my friends carefully, and I learned a lot from Dr. Ague Draven."

Picking up on the reference to Ague's ability to read people through touch, my eyes bulge. I do a double-take of both Brynlee and Mayhem. "Okay, I accept that, Brynlee," I say. "But she's—and I mean no offence, Mayhem—but she's a teenager."

Fin clears her throat. "In age, maybe, but remember where she grew up. She gets street credit added to her age."

My memory jumps to my introduction to Tawny—one of the other three crows—and how she described meeting Blake and Mayhem on the streets when Blake was four and Mayhem was six. They became the three crows. Mayhem was fierce and protective; I believe Tawny used the words "rabid animal" to describe Mayhem. I purse my lips and close my eyes. *We could use that kind of passion. Mayhem's "street credit" suggestions she'll act with caution. Hopefully, her lack of intimate or personal connection with Cian, Dodo, or Ague will take the recklessness out of her decisions.* "Welcome to the team, Mayhem."

"Coffee?" Fin asks. She's already filling mugs. The milk, vanilla creamer, sugar, and a bottle of Kahlua are set out in the centre of the breakfast bar. Fin then grabs a box of cookies from the cupboard, dumps them on a plate, and plops the plate next to the coffee fixings. We gather, all feeling Dodo's absence.

I reposition close to the breakfast bar and pick up a cookie. It's hard and heavy. I tap it on the counter. It clicks without crumbling or breaking. *Store-bought cookies can't compare to Dodo's homemade ones.* I take a tentative nibble. It's grainy and dry. It grinds in my teeth and I need a gulp of coffee to wash it down. I sit the rest down, uneaten. I'm about to launch into an update for Brynlee and Mayhem when Fin hops off the stool and heads toward her bedroom.

"Thought of something I need to do," she mumbles, slamming her bedroom door.

I raise an eyebrow, but otherwise don't worry about what Fin might do. Griffin is here after all, so that suggests—knowing Fin—that she's doing something sexy.

I update Brynlee and Mayhem. They listen attentively. When I'm done, we decide to call it a night and set a plan for entering the tunnels in the morning.

Chapter 12

Strange noises came from Fin's room most of last night, and they were not the intimate sounds that usually come from her room when Griffin is home. These noises were of the mumbling, shuffling, tapping, and clattering variety. How Griffin, or anybody else, got any sleep is beyond me. I put my earplugs in when it became apparent that she had no intention of sleeping. So, I've no idea what time her bedroom adventures shut down.

I'm the first person in the kitchen this morning. Being the first is an unusual experience, and Dodo's loss washes over me again. I'm glad for a few moments alone. Although Dodo didn't live here, he liked to pop in on tiptoe in the morning and start our coffee for us. Sometimes, depending on what he was cooking for the breakfast customers at Just Flavours when he opened the café, he'd leave us breakfast, too.

I focus on brewing the coffee, turning the act into a mindful grounding moment before this day starts. I'm standing, staring at the coffeemaker and listening to it sputter and gurgle when I hear the floor creak. Glancing up, I observe a haggard-looking Fin. "Did you sleep?" I ask. Surveying her, I add, "Are you naked?"

Fin gazes down the length of her body, which is coated in an array of paint colours—not edible, judging by the acrylic scent. She looks up at me and scrubs her face with her hand. "I'm wearing paint and underwear, Kori. Don't be ridiculous. Do you think that I'd wander around naked when we have company?"

I raise my eyebrows and pull my lips into a questioning curl. She waves a hand at me and sashays off to the bathroom.

"Um, Fin. What do you plan on wearing out of the bathroom?"

She pops her head out of the doorway with a glowing smile. "My bare skin."

I blow out a breath and snatch the coffeepot off the burner. I can't wait for it to finish brewing. The coffeemaker makes a hiss and sizzle combo as the water drips onto the hotplate and becomes a puff of steam.

"That kind of morning?" Belamey asks, coming into the room and stretching. He's clutching his T-shirt in his hand. His black tracker pants hang low on his hips, and his toned stomach taunts me. He scratches his stomach, winks at me, and pulls his shirt on. "Going to be another morning where Fin does her naked dash, is it?" He chuckles.

I set my cup on the counter and pour Belamey a mugful. We sip in silence, finishing our first coffees of the day at the same time. I reach for the pot and refill our mugs. "Fin said I was ridiculous for suggesting she'd be naked in a house full of company." I find a small smile tugging at the corners of my mouth.

Before Belamey picks up his fresh mug, he grabs me by the hips and pulls me close. When I turn my face up in surprise, he rests his lips on mine with a soft kiss that leaves me breathless. He releases me and picks up his mug. "Last week, she stood at the breakfast bar nude and poured herself a coffee to take to her room to get dressed." He takes a sip of his coffee.

"There was hardly anybody here," Fin says, emerging from the bathroom. A tropical coconut scent wafts out with her, a combo of her shampoo, soap, and body cream.

Belamey chuckles but keeps his gaze angled at his mug. I'm surprised by the towel Fin is holding in front of her.

Brynlee and Mayhem enter the kitchen from the living room. Fin doesn't stop for a coffee. "I'll be right back. Can you pour me a mug, please?"

Brynlee gasps and her eyes go wide as Fin walks by them. Mayhem's mouth falls open. They both stand where they are, staring in Fin's direction even after we hear her door close. Mayhem turns her head to Belamey. "You keep strange friends, Bel."

I'm surprised by Mayhem's shortening of Belamey's name, and I reconsider the nature of their relationship.

Belamey was a mentor to Dodo. He saved him from a darker fate. I peer toward Mayhem. *She's like a little sister he'd try to protect. But Mayhem isn't the type to let anyone protect her.* I watch as they interact for a few minutes. *Mutual respect.*

Fin and Griffin come into the room. Fin is clothed in camo cargo pants and a black T-shirt, which isn't overly dramatic. The part that takes her outfit over the top is all the knives she's strapped to herself. She's a master at knife throwing, a skill she gained when the Ember stone surfaced and her ability to see the Spellbinders' world of magic awoke. She loves carrying knives on her body—legal or not. Today, she's overzealous. There are knives on her biceps, a loaded knife belt around her waist, and four thin—but fully loaded—belts around her thighs, two strapped around each thigh.

My eyes rotate to the top of my head.

"Kori Anise Regan Ember," Fin gives me one of my signature foot stomps. "You, of all people, know how savage those tunnels are."

I have my lips sucked in and pinched together. "Finley Sophia Salinger," I fire at her, then the playfulness drains from my voice. "You'll need those knives coated with magic."

"I got that," Griffin says before his face disappears behind his coffee. He's more rested than I expected, given he sleeps in Fin's room.

I flash him a half-hearted smile.

"Either of you ever been in the tunnels?" Belamey asks Brynlee and Mayhem. They meet his question with head shakes and unsure faces.

"Well, let me tell you," Fin says. "It's like hell is closer to the surface than we thought."

"Thanks, Fin. That's not scary at all," Brynlee says.

Mayhem pushes her shoulders back and lengthens her spine. "I've lived in hell, so let's just get this over with."

Fin is stepping from foot to foot. "Do you think this section of the tunnels will be the same as the others?"

"I have zero expectations at all, Fin. It's just easier that way," I say. "Does anyone have Rye's book with the tunnel mapping? It might have some or all of that area mapped out." I sigh at the negative response.

"Different areas of the tunnels are guarded based on who once controlled them," Belamey reminds us.

I scrunch my face. "Or, I guess, who currently controls them." *Supposedly, the tunnels haven't been common knowledge in decades, but that assumption might need to be re-evaluated.*

"What do we need to know before we go in? Is there anything that might prepare us?" Mayhem asks.

"Well, here's what we were told. The unfortunate part for us was that we were already in the tunnels." Fin grimaces. "We were informed by a faerie, but that's a story f—"

"Fin?" Brynlee cuts in, familiar with the way Fin can get off track.

"We were advised," Fin pauses and waggles her tongue at Brynlee, "there are strange things that can only be found in the tunnels. Creations—mutated creatures or something—used to guard the tunnels or things in them. So, go in expecting to die, and you *might* come out."

Brynlee is scowling at Fin. Mayhem is nodding, and she has a genuine grin on her face. Her tone of voice is light. "Excellent. How do we get in?"

Belamey, Griffin, Fin, and I exchange glances.

"Seriously? You don't know how we get in?" Brynlee drops a piece of bread into the toaster. Her back is to us, so I can't weigh her expression.

"Oh, we know a few ways to get in, smarty-pants." Fin puts her hands in her pocket and rocks on her heels. "It's just that it's best to enter the tunnels as close as possible to the location we want to visit to avoid unnatural terror, having our blood sucked from our bodies through a creature's tongue, other cruel terminations of life, and various plagues of death. You know, the basic grievances."

I shoot Fin a shut-up stare. "What our dramatic friend is trying to say is that we know places to enter the tunnels within reasonable proximity to The Society of the Blood Wind house. But those are too far from the area under the super jail, which is out on Highway 36."

"We need a secretary bird," Belamey says, rubbing his chin.

"I know one. I'll go talk with him," Griffin says. "It's not far. Eat, have another cup of coffee, and for those of you who aren't dressed . . ." He crosses the kitchen and opens the window while speaking.

"Remember, nobody goes anywhere alone," Belamey says.

"I agree." Fin points at Griffin. "Especially you. Particular people in this room are likely next on a certain psychopath's snatch-and-grab list."

Griffin closes the window.

Fin hops up. "I'll drive."

I race to get dressed, and we pile into the Bronco. Just Griffin and Fin are in the cab. The rest of us settle in the box. When our short drive concludes, we're at a dead-end street with a chain-link fence marking no exit. It's the same fence I hopped to get to the abandoned factory where I almost died fighting Adria Blaze a few months ago. That feels so far away. It was winter then. Now, with summer in full swing, the handful of deteriorating houses on this street are overgrown. Places for seedy individuals to hide are plentiful.

As we trudge down the street behind Griffin, the strong, sweet smell coming from the lilac bushes contrasts with the rundown state of our surroundings. My eyes don't stop scanning for threats. Griffin leads us through knee-high grass toward a once-white house. He holds his hand up and closes it into a fist, indicating we need to stop. He gives a series of whistles that I perceive as coded, and we wait.

The quilled head of a secretary bird pops out of the foliage and fixes us with its bright-orange-rimmed eyes. It tips its head to the side. I assume it recognizes Griffin because the bird transforms into a scruffy, skinny man with a black toque yanked down so low it covers his eyebrows; he must have missed the seasonal change. "What do you want, Griff?" His tone is unimpressed and impatient.

"We need access to the underground, old friend."

The man grunts, wipes his hands on his dirt-stained jeans, and holds out his hand.

Griffin approaches him and places something in the man's hand. Payment of some sort.

They exchange no more words as the man becomes a bird and starts walking to the rear of the property. Griffin waves at us to follow. We plow through the grass and struggle through a straggly crop of trees that may have been lilac trees at one point but are now a dead tangle of branches.

We push our way into a clearing that requires us to fan out sideways in a circle around a raised cement well. I'm up against the trees, and the branches are clinging to me. Trying to ignore the creeping feeling that rises inside me, I watch as Griffin heaves the cover off the top of the well.

Chapter 13

I step forward first—I don't know why—and lean over the edge, peering into the darkness below. The odour of damp, uncirculated air is the first thing I notice. I grimace and close my eyes. After a moment, I pop them open again and search for the narrow ledge and winding stone stairs that circle the well, but that isn't how this entrance was constructed. Instead, on the inside wall is a ladder so flimsy that it looks like it wouldn't even hold the weight of a spider. I straighten and rub my palm on my forehead. "You can't be serious?"

"What?" Fin bumps me to the side so she has a line of sight. She stands and flashes a fake smile in Griffin's direction. "He's lost it," she whispers to me out of the corner of her mouth. "The stress must be getting to him."

I raise my eyebrows at her and purse my lips. I turn away from the well. "This is the closest we can get?" I glance diagonally in the jail's general direction, and when everyone else follows my gaze, I talk again. "Walking above ground, if we had a direct path between here and the jail is about two kilometres. That would be about a thirty-minute walk. Based on our previous experience in the tunnels, our path to the jail won't be direct or easy walking."

"Half an hour underground can feel like a lifetime," Fin whispers.

Griffin nods, but it's unclear if his nod is for mine or Fin's comment. When he speaks, it's to the group. "I don't have any other contacts for the tunnels. Does anybody else?" He studies Belamey, who shrugs. Brynlee and Mayhem are shaking their heads no.

"Alright then. Have you been in this area of the tunnels, Griffin?" I ask.

"No."

I grimace. "We'll need to go down one at a time." My tone is light. "I'll go in first."

"Look at the bright side, Kori." Fin pipes up. "If the ladder pulls away from the wall, it's only going to bang against the side. But if you fall to your death, then at least you won't have to travel through these nightmare-ish tunnels." She pauses. "Oh, and death by falling seems like a better alternative than being murdered by a psycho."

I don't even dignify Fin's ramble with a glance in her direction. Flipping a leg over the edge, I feel for the first rung of the ladder.

"I'm right behind you, Firecracker," Belamey says.

It takes a bit of effort to muster a nod and swallow the lump in my throat. I put my shield on and begin my descent. The cross bars are rounded and feel like pieces of wood a rodent gnawed on. Tiny slivers poke into my skin. The ladder protests with creaks and croaks. Each rung I step on has a bit of give, so my climb is slow as I wait to see if my foothold is going to fail. After a while, I can't hear the conversation at the top of the well. When I glance up, the light is dim; I'm way farther down than I thought.

My foot is swinging, toes pointed, trying to find the next rung or the ground. I can't feel anything. The ladder groans, and I peer up. Nothing is visible, but I get the sense that Belamey has entered the well. *I need off this ladder.* I form a dim light orb and lower my hand. "Smoke and ashes," I hiss. "The bottom half of the ladder is missing," I yell, my head tilted up. I look down and drop my orb. It seems to drop forever, and the ground isn't visible. "It's just because it was such a dim orb," I whisper to myself.

I keep one foot on the bottom rung and one dangling in the air. Pushing my buttocks out, I reach toward the bottom rung with my hands. I shake my head at myself. *This is suicide.* I take my other foot off the rung and hang from it. My toes hit the wall of the well, but don't find any ground. I'm committed now, though.

Dropping, I grunt as I hit the ground, my hands coming down in front of me. Beneath my palms, the ground is damp and squishy. My orb is gone, having dissipated with time and distance from me. I stay crouched and form another pale light orb. The fearful instructions from the last time we were in the tunnels roll in my brain. *Faint lighting is the safest choice in tunnels where you don't know what might sleep; sleeping creatures are best left asleep.*

Encouraged that nothing has attacked me, I stand and move from under the ladder so Belamey doesn't drop on top of me. My laborious breathing echoes in the otherwise silent space. My eyes continue to drift up, eager for someone to join me. *Why did I volunteer to come down first?*

I move the light and count four exits. One tunnel has the dim glow of bewitchment sparkles. Another tunnel is a narrow cylinder shape all the way along, at least as far as I can see. It doesn't change shape or get wider at all.

"Kori?" Belamey's voice echoes in the well even though he's lowered his volume.

"Hang and drop. The ground isn't that far down. I think it's less than ten feet, but you have to hang first to shorten the fall or you'll injure yourself."

Belamey's shadowed form drops. He straightens, dusting himself off. He doesn't create any form of magic light but looks around. "Would've been ideal if one of the entrances ran in the jail's direction. I think we need to go that way." He points between the two tunnels I haven't looked closely at yet.

"Agreed." I point to the tunnel that goes away from where we want to go. "It would've been nice if one of the two tunnels we have to choose from was lined with that sparkling light. At least we would have known what the danger was."

Fin drops in, and I jump. "Blazing hell, Fin."

Fin turns in a circle and focuses where I was pointing. "Oh, bewitchment sparkles." She steps toward the opening of that tunnel. "Their lure is terrifying and powerful, but turning into a beautiful crystalized statue isn't the worst death imaginable." She spins toward me. "Can you remind me—if we don't die—that I borrowed a book from Grama Pearle about Evanora Trevils, the evil Spellbinder credited with creating the sparkles? It's called *The Trevils Legends*."

I can feel the *are you kidding me expression* on my face. "Sure, Fin."

"We're going to need to pick one of these tunnels and move into it because we have three more people coming down that ladder, and we don't have enough space." Belamey's voice is muffled because he's facing the wall in the middle of the two tunnels and looking back and forth between them.

"No problem," Fin says. "I know how to choose." She brushes past me and stands on Belamey's left, shoulder to shoulder. Her hand is fishing in the cargo pocket on her left side. I can't determine what she pulls out and puts in front of her, but there are two cracks and a faint glow. Her head turns toward Belamey. "Glow sticks, the normie orbs." She giggles. "Normie orb. I should patent that." She's watching Belamey when she tosses one glow stick into the left tunnel and another into the right.

The glow sticks make a modest thump when they hit the ground. We can make out their glow, but Fin threw them too far in for us to make out anything near them. "Blazing hell, Fin." I'm holding my breath, unsure of what to expect.

"I'm not going into a tunnel that might have murk salamanders, murk monsters, or whatever you want to call them. I've no desire to be hunted in the dark by a creature that is so accustomed to living in the darkness that it doesn't need eyes! Plus, I don't want to die with a tongue burrowed in my flesh, draining my bodily fluids."

I hiss at her, "Would you stop referring to dea—"

The click of a murk monster cuts me off. My blood runs cold. Fin and Belamey step away from the two openings, crowding us together in the well's centre. I analyze the distance between the ground and where I imagine the ladder to be above us, wondering if we could leap for the rungs. *Not a chance.* "Did you have to call attention to one of the hardest things to kill, Fin?" My voice pitches with anger and fear.

Fin's voice is a whisper. "Murk monsters are bonded to the tunnels connected to the well entrances, remember?"

I'm having trouble controlling the volume of my voice. "Yes, but does that mean they can come *into* the entrance?"

"We're about to find out," Belamey says, magic sparking to light on his hands.

Casting a dome over us, I pray it's tight enough against the dirt. I can't remember if these creatures can dig. I form an orb that won't affect us, but the orb will hopefully overwhelm the murk monster's sharpened senses with its sound, smell, and vibrations. Waiting, I hold it.

At the entrance to the left tunnel, low to the ground, the head of a murk monster appears. It's a dark shadow. If you weren't searching for it, it would be easy to assume it was a trick of the low light. In the darkness, you wouldn't see it all. This one, based on its head size, is big enough to eat us whole. It's clicking, calling for others. Another clicks in response. A petite salamander materializes beside the bigger one. Its tail is pointed straight up, and it's screeching. They aren't moving, but their limbs are tense.

"I have to release the dome," I mumble. "If someone drops on top, they might slide to their death."

Belamey's head is moving up and down, but Fin answers. "They can't come in. Check them out. They're waiting to pounce."

I drop the dome.

"Don't be so sure, Fin. They're sneaky and, as you pointed out, they're waiting to spring." Belamey's voice is tense.

Something drops from above, brushing down the length of my backside. I yell and stumble forward, barely keeping from knocking Fin and Belamey into the murk monster. Hands tighten on my shoulders. "It's me, cousin. Why are you standing under the ladder? You're lucky I didn't land on your . . ." Brynlee's voice fades as she gets a view of the creatures watching us.

"Don't ask for details," Fin says over her shoulder. "Just know that it's a death we don't want to experience. The thing is, we don't think they can enter this room."

Brynlee's voice cracks. "Don't think?"

Nobody answers her because the ladder's groan is loud, like it's tired of supporting people's weight. "It would be nice if people would announce their arrival before dropping in," I grumble.

"Most people don't stand under a ladder when they know other people are using it," Fin says.

She makes a fair point. I shrug. "We need to move."

"Guess we know which tunnel to pick." Fin smirks. None of us give voice to the fact that we have no idea what's in the right-hand tunnel.

"I'll watch them," Belamey says. "You guys enter the next tunnel."

My eyes feel dry from not blinking. My skin is clammy, and my hands are shaking as I move toward the entrance on the right of Belamey. Brynlee's hand is holding the top of my shoulder like we're performing a police room-clearing exercise. Jaw clenched and fighting claustrophobia, I step into the tunnel. I hold my breath. When no clicking starts ahead of me, and nothing drops on me or otherwise attacks, I let my breath out. We move ten paces forward and stop. Brynlee pushes her back against mine.

My orb shows we are entering a tight space with roots growing through the roof and walls. The ground under my feet is still dirt, but in a few more steps, it's uneven and peppered with holes where the roots cover the ground. There's no apparent danger yet, but my senses are heightened, and I'm on full alert.

It feels like an impossible amount of time passes

while we wait for Mayhem and Griffin to drop into the well. When Belamey calls out that we're all in the tunnel and ready to go, I'm not sure if my fear lowers because of the success of our first stage of this mission or intensifies because we now have to move forward into a tunnel that's concealing danger from us.

Chapter 14

With my eyes fixed on the ground to avoid tripping on the roots, I lead us deeper into the tunnel. As we move, I feel a growing apprehension. The roots have a snake-like quality, and I can't get past the feeling that it's more than a trick of the light creating the illusion. "Guys, something doesn't feel right to me." I keep my volume hushed and my feet moving. *This is too easy.* I rub my arm with my free hand. "There has to be something we aren't seeing."

Because there are six of us moving through the tunnel, the faint light from my orb isn't enough to assist the people near the rear of our group. When I glance back, I see Griffin, at our tail end, has created an orb similar to mine. Fear prickles my skin when I hear Griffin grunt in response to whatever he's viewing.

"Griff?" Belamey hisses.

"Just keep moving and don't stop. If something gets in your way, blast it with magic and charge right through."

A blast orb forms in my other hand, and I infuse it with a faint glow. My shoulders curl forward and my neck is bent, straining for a glimpse of whatever might present us with danger. My hands shake slightly, and a sheen of sweat breaks out on my forehead. I hear Griffin saying something, but he's too far away and speaking too low for me to make out the words.

"Holy snot balls," Fin says in a voice that's too loud for our situation. Her elaborate response to Griffin's words does nothing to ease my nerves.

"Kori," Fin calls in a loud whisper. I hear a commotion and grunting.

"Watch it," Brynlee hisses.

Mayhem's words have a muted anger. "Ouch, shit Fin!"

"Move over, Belamey." Fin's voice has moved closer and then it's right behind me. Squeezing past three people in this narrow space would've been a feat of balance and grace if everyone's grumbling didn't accompany it. She doesn't sound abashed. Her tone is high-pitched and shaky. "Kori, don't stop moving."

"Yeah. I received those instructions already, Fin."

"The vines are alive!"

I almost trip on a high-growing root. "What?"

"If you look closely, you can see them moving in a subtle slither." She pauses, and I imagine her head moving as she scans these new dangers surrounding us, contemplating their light grey roots. "They aren't fast-moving, so we're fine as long as we don't stop. If we stop, the roots capture us, and we become tangled in them. It's next to impossible to escape once they catch you." She falls silent.

I reconsider the roots, which are shaped oddly. They feel firm underfoot with a slight give. The air smells of damp soil with a hint of decay. But what I mistook for a trick of the light is a twisting slide motion that allows damp areas of the root system to move into the air to breathe.

"These roots grow from some ancient . . . plant . . . creature," Fin huffs. "They grow up from whatever they're attached to farther down." I slow, but Fin doesn't, and her feet clip my heels, pulling at the heel of my shoe. "Keep moving," she says. She puts her hands on my shoulder blades, trying to increase my speed to match hers.

"Look," I growl at her. I risk turning my head to the side to see her peeking over my shoulder.

"Blast, and keep moving."

I know she's right. If we stop here, the few people in front might get to safety, but we would trap the end ones. A change in the tunnel is close, but to reach it, we need to get through a web that resembles nothing a normal-sized spider would make. I work my tongue in my mouth, desperate to create moisture. My eyes work overtime, trying to find the creator of this network of glistening fibres. We're getting closer, and I don't want to risk finding out how sticky the netting is. I switch my orb to a supercharged air orb and launch it forward.

The orb creates a sucking noise in the narrow tunnel

and tears through the web, dragging strings of it farther down the tunnel as it blows. I drop a dome over me and Fin so we can pass through the area without fear of a spider or anything else dropping on us. I trust the people behind us will take some kind of precaution in response to seeing me do it.

Fin and I charge past the spot where the web once hung. We move a decent distance into the tunnel and away from the roots before we stop to wait for the others. I search for threats. We're in a crumbling stone section with a hard-packed dirt floor and no roots. The air is stale but not rank. Fin manages to speak with cheerful tones. "No bats in eternal sleep and no murk monsters."

I crack my neck from side to side, but don't respond. It's wide enough to walk two abreast, so we pair off. Fin moves back to walk with Griffin. Belamey and Mayhem are discussing something, so Brynlee takes the place beside me. We continue forward in silence. We've gone thirty feet when we come to a fork. In the lead with Brynlee, I angle us into the left tunnel. My logic is that we need to cut back a bit to head in the jail's direction, which I noted before we entered the tunnels. Nobody objects, and we keep moving.

"Do you hear that?" I whisper to Brynlee.

"The indistinct squeaks? Yes."

"Do you know what's making it?"

"Nope."

"Under different circumstances, I'd relate those noises to mice." I scratch my head. "But here . . ." Dull scratching and shuffling join the squeaks. I squint into the darkness ahead of us. Low to the ground is a round, blue-green light the size of a grape. "Do you see it?" I ask Brynlee.

Her head bobs. We move with caution. My goal is to go past it without incident. As we near it, it stays in one spot—glowing and unmoving. It's fascinating how it just hangs there, suspended in the air. I almost don't notice when Brynlee stops. As I pause and turn, she bends to get closer to it. Mayhem, in a blur, shoulder checks Brynlee, who sails sideways and lands with a grunt on her side in the dirt. Our group stops.

"Burning brimstone, Mayhem!" I move to help Brynlee to her feet.

"You must be an amazing rugby player," Fin comments, taking the actions of the last few seconds in stride.

Mayhem is standing in front of the glow but closer to the opposite wall. She has her hands out to the left and right of her body to caution us to stay away. She assesses to make sure we're heeding her warning before dropping her arms and creating a bright light orb, which she drops. It spins over the ground toward the glow.

My mouth falls open. The light has revealed what resembles a reddish-brown deer mouse with a black underbelly. It's sitting on its haunches with its dark grey front feet held out in front of it. But its lengthy tail is curled up over its body with the glowing ball of flesh— a lure. It doesn't appear deadly or even threatening, but I understand that's the point. Its glowing lure is to attract its prey.

"Watch." Mayhem creates another orb, just a ball, that she drops. It rolls toward the little mouse imposter but stops a few inches away. The creature opens its mouth and a forked tongue the colour of the lure shoots out, puncturing the orb. Its tongue moves back into its mouth, and the creature waits, its bulging eyes focused on the orb.

"What the f—"

I cut Fin off. "Mayhem, what in the fiery blazes is that thing?"

"Rodent of the abyss. We need to move. Sometimes they travel solo, but sometimes . . ." Mayhem lets her sentence drop off. I don't need to be told twice. I hook Brynlee's arm and drag her with me.

"Mayhem, I need to know more," Fin says. I can hear our group's feet moving down the tunnel in a steady rhythm.

"I saw a dead one once, a long time ago. The street kid who had it told stories of these creatures that lived deep beneath the ground in tunnels. Creatures that hunt by drawing prey in with a glow that's attached to their bodies. When the prey is close enough, they paralyze them with venom injected from their tongue. They wait and then eat you while you're alive." She clears her throat. "They like the eyes. Your best hope is that there'll be a swarm, so you die quicker."

"Forget I asked," Fin says, gagging.

We make it through the length of the tunnel with no more rodents of the abyss, or anything else untold, appearing, but then the tunnel abruptly changes direction. It goes straight up—a rock wall. The indents and protrusions make it clear what we need to do next.

It's so dark when I look up that it's impossible to know how high we need to climb. The opening is tight, though. If we need a break while climbing, and are brave enough to recline, we can brace ourselves between the walls.

"I'll go first this time," Belamey says, mounting the wall.

"I'll take the rear," Griffin says. He turns to watch down the tunnel.

"You just want to watch my rear," Fin says without trying to make the comment private. Griffin chuckles.

I mount the wall after Belamey. The holes aren't big enough for more than the toe of a shoe. The handholds are jagged and slippery with loose dirt and dust. "This will be fun," I mumble sarcastically. If any of us are thinking about mutated creatures or insects, we're keeping those thoughts to ourselves—even Fin.

I move repetitively; foot up, push, reach for a hold. The top of the ledge comes faster than I expected, and it's lit with a mellow glow. *Bewitchment sparkles, like the first tunnel I noticed when I dropped into the well.* Belamey grabs my arms and hoists me over the lip into a new tunnel. The sparkles coat the walls of this tunnel, but thankfully not the floor, as far as I can see. I feel the pull, a deep longing to just touch the pretty sparkles, sparkles that crystallize anything that touches them.

"Excellent," I huff. I'm angry with the drain resisting the sparkles will have on everybody's energy. I move to the edge and peer down to focus on something other than the bewitchment sparkles.

The others can't finish the climb fast enough for me. I'm vibrating, trying to resist the sparkles. No explanation of this danger is needed; their beguiling lure is well known in the Spellbinder world, and this isn't our first experience with them. So, as soon as I see the top of Griffin's head, I turn and power forward, fighting the compulsion to touch anything. I break into a run. I need to get past this section. My heart is pounding, and I'm panting with the exertion of the run and the resistance to initiating my crystalizing demise.

I skid to a stop, pinwheeling my arms. A round door is closed in front of me. The group crowds in behind me. Griffin casts a dome over us with a weave I've never seen before. The dome insulates us from the desire to touch the walls, but it only lessens the urge a tiny amount. He's standing with his backside to us, keeping vigilance down the hall.

"Get it open!" Fin's voice is high-pitched. "Is it warded? Why are we stopping? Holy man, the walls are so pretty."

The door has a thick round bullring in the centre, which I assume is a knocker. Brynlee pushes past me and grabs the ring. She leans back, using her total body weight to pull it. It gives a tiny bit, and she juts backwards an inch. Her voice is stilted. "Need help to turn the handle," she says.

Bclamcy moves up behind her, bracing his body around her, and places his hands on the ring on either side of hers.

"To . . . the . . . right." The strength she's exerting is heavy in her words.

Belamey is grunting with his efforts. I want to help, but there isn't enough room for me.

"So pretty," Fin says. The change in her voice scares me.

The door gives way, and Belamey and Brynlee let go, falling to the floor just short of the door ramming them into the wall. This is happening on my right as I catch sight of Fin bending and reaching for the sparkles.

"NOOO!" I dive for her, but I'm too far away.

Chapter 15

I dive through the spot where Fin should've been, either as a human or a crystalized statue. I skid across the dirt floor on my stomach, the grit and stones tearing at the skin of my palms. The sparkle-covered wall is a few inches from the side of my body. I come to a stop, spitting grime from my mouth beside Griffin. He scowls down and then over his shoulder.

Gazing up from my vantage point on the floor, I watch Griffin's chest puff out with an audible sigh. His response suggests that Fin is okay. I roll toward Griffin enough to get space to stand without bumping the wall. Brushing dirt off the front of my body, I turn and spot Fin. She's lying on her back in the middle of the tunnel. Her eyes are opening and closing, and she's gasping for air. Mayhem is draped diagonally over Fin's body. Closer than I was to Fin, Mayhem had reached her first.

"Rug . . . by," Fin gasps. "You should . . . play . . . rugby."

Mayhem stands and brushes herself off when I'm close enough to reach my hand down to Fin. I yank her up, noting that Brynlee and Belamey are on their feet again, too. Our temporary chaos had muddled the lure of the sparkles, but now that things are returning to normal, I'm aware of the pull, like the sparkles are magnetized and I'm the magnet. The power of them never diminishes.

"Through the door!" Belamey hollers. He and Brynlee are leaning their backs against the door. The door is shoving them forward, trying to close. There has to be a mechanism powering the door. Their heels are grinding into the ground, and small mounds of debris are forming in front of them.

"Dome is down," Griffin advises as he joins us.

I grab Fin and drag her with me. I'm on Mayhem's heels. We pile through the door, and Belamey and Brynlee hop away from it, allowing it to swing shut. Everyone is present and appears to be in one piece except for my skinned hands. I glance at my wristwatch, guesstimating the distance between the well we entered and the jail we're trying to reach. "We have to be pretty close now." I let my eyes explore the tunnel we're in.

The floor is black slate, with the same tiles covering the walls and the ceiling. There's no shine; it's a stark contrast to the tunnel we just left behind. There's no light except the orbs Mayhem and I are now holding. The tunnel has a chill to it that's dry instead of damp.

There are no visible threads of magic in my line of sight. I turn to the door and my pulse spikes.

"Is everyone okay?" My voice is shrill. I spin so I'm facing the group and the door. "There's a broken hex on that door. Who was through it firs—"

The light orb in Mayhem's hand increases in intensity and rolls with flames. Her eyes are unblinking as she stares at the fireball in her hand.

"Shit!" I throw a dome up around us, leaving Mayhem out. Fire slams into the dome in front of my face and breaks apart. Flames of red, orange, and yellow spin over the dome, fizzling out into thick streams of smoke. Another fire orb hits the dome.

"Tell me we can help her," Fin says. "She can't stay one of Nyoka's pawns forever."

"I need to get close to her," Brynlee says, her voice unsure. I survey Brynlee to confirm if what I hear in her voice is present in her features and to make sure she isn't bewitched. Her eyes are fixed on Mayhem. Her shoulders are back, chest high, chin thrust out. "I need to get close to Mayhem," she repeats. This time, it's a firm command. She walks toward the edge of the dome, her steps steady.

I move with her so that she stays under the dome's protection. Mayhem doesn't stray from her spot. Fire regenerates in her hand, and she throws it.

"It's a very one-dimensional curse. If she were alone or managed to kill everyone travelling with her, she'd be stuck repeating this action until she dies." Brynlee whispers. Whether consciously or unconsciously, her proximity to Mayhem causes her to lower her voice.

The broken hex didn't appear basic to me.

"Don't panic," she says, with no sign of whom she's talking to. Without warning, she jumps from the safety of the dome, timing her movement with the regeneration of a round of fire, and launches herself to Mayhem's side. Brynlee wastes no time moving behind Mayhem.

If Mayhem is aware, she doesn't show it. I can see Brynlee's mouth moving, though I can't hear any words. Brynlee's hands come into view, moving overtop of Mayhem's head before dipping behind her head again. Brynlee fits a tight weave of magic down over Mayhem's head. It's clear, so Mayhem's face remains visible to us. Mayhem pauses, blinks for the first time since we realized she was cursed, and then continues to launch fire at us. Underneath our dome feels hot, but not from the fire orbs—my dome protects us from the orb's heat as well. We are packed close together, and the heat is coming from our bodies; we're charged with adrenalin and sweating from it.

Brynlee's hands move fast over Mayhem's head. She even dares to make the movements in front of Mayhem's face. Mayhem's eyes are glazed and focusing on something else, anyway. Regardless, we don't know how she'll respond. Mayhem's body convulses in response to whatever Brynlee is doing. My mouth drops open when grey smoke comes off Mayhem's body. The smoke twists together and snakes up toward her head.

"Can anyone else see this?" I ask, unsure if I'm observing a weave of magic or actual smoke.

"That is shit-ass creepy stuff going on," Fin says, her

words slow, but a confirmation that she can see what I'm seeing.

I nod and close my mouth. The smoke twines are weaving in and out of Mayhem's body, and she's still convulsing. When they dip in at her neckline, we don't view them come out again, but the clear magic bag on Mayhem's head fills with snake-like cords of smoke. They writhe.

Because the bag is clear, we can see the smoke building up around her head area. The smoke snakes are wild, and the colour surrounding Mayhem's head is a storm-cloud shade. Her eyes close, her hand drops, and she releases the fire magic she was holding. The convulsing stops as well, and there's no more smoke coming out of her body.

I leave the dome in place, unsure.

Brynlee fits her hands around Mayhem's neck and leans in, her mouth close to Mayhem's skin, whispering. Brynlee's words stop, and she blows air onto her hands where they connect with Mayhem's neck. With a burst of speed, she moves her hands out and up, pulling the bag off Mayhem's head. Brynlee grips the bag closed, trapping the ash-grey smoke, before she ties it and sets it gingerly on the floor. "Anybody object to leaving this hex here?"

Nobody objects.

"Where did you learn that?" I'm impressed with Brynlee's ability to remove the hex on Mayhem and a bit scared of her power—her magical abilities are growing.

"Ague." Brynlee says, her tone implying that I

shouldn't ask ridiculous questions.

Mayhem blinks and sucks a gulp of air. She wets her lips before she speaks. "I . . . I had no control. I was aware of what I was doing, but I was powerless to stop." She shivers. I drop the dome, but Fin has already charged through it to hug Mayhem.

"I don't see any other magic clinging to this space," I say eventually.

"Nyoka is prideful and ignorant. So, I'd say there won't be any more," Belamey answers in his husky voice.

"And creatures?" I consider the space and the door before answering my question. "She's claimed this space, cleared it of anything like the murk monsters and rodents of the abyss." I sigh. *Are we in more danger now than we were in the other tunnels?*

We travel through the tunnel in silence. Because we think we're getting close to the jail and where we suspect Kyson and Nyoka might hide, I magically amplify my hearing as a precaution. It alerts me to voices ahead, where the light changes farther down the tunnel. If this area is anything like the tunnels under The Society of the Blood Wind house, then we're coming up on an open space, as close as it gets to a room in these underground chambers.

Using a complex meshwork that uses light and air to hide the physical body and its sounds, smells, and, to some extent, magic—masking—we risk getting closer. From this distance, I can hear voices without using magic. We're all masked, except Fin, who we've positioned farther back in the tunnel, so she's less likely to be seen. I can make out a woman's voice and assume it's Nyoka, especially since she's arguing with Kyson. There are three other voices I don't recognize.

A voice that booms like thunder in the underground space forms the first sentence we can hear properly. "Do I look inferior, witch?"

High-pitched giggling parrots, "Do I look inferior?" It's hard to tell if this is hysteria at work or insanity. "Do I look in—"

"Shut up, idiot," Kyson cuts in. "Nyoka?" He makes her name a question.

The same booming voice, whom Belamey identifies as Ruck, announces he's leaving to complete "Mission Capture." *Capture who? One of us?* My heartbeat races, my nose flares, and my jaw clenches. Thoughts of Ague and Dodo's deaths fill my brain. The smell of decomposition—a smell familiar to a seasoned cop—clogs my nasal passage, and even the imagined odour makes my stomach roll. I close my eyes and focus on the hard ground under my feet. *You're imagining the smell. Everyone with you is alive.*

"I am in control here, Alaster Ruckus. Not you and not him." The voice is female, the same voice that was arguing with Kyson moments before. It's stern and carries an energy to it that sends chills down my spine and brings me back to the present moment.

"Nyoka Cifarelli," I whisper to myself. I have a strange eagerness to see what this terrifying woman looks like.

"Don't look at Kyson, Alaster," she hisses. "He knows his place. Don't you, kitten?"

A low growl is the only response. I assume it's Kyson,

not Ruck, because it isn't deep. The high-pitched giggle starts again, followed by what I assume is a mocking of the growl, but it sounds more like a human screeching. Kyson's voice is threatening, "Shut your nutball sister up, you birdbrain, or—"

I tally the voices in my head—Ruck's booming voice, Kyson's grating voice, Nyoka's stern one, a giggling Spellbinder, and the giggler's brother. That's five.

"It's time anyway," Nyoka says. There are three distinct grunts—a resonant one, a squeaking one, and another, perhaps from the Spellbinder referred to as "bird brain." There is no sound proceeding the grunts, and silence follows. My body is tense as I look at my companions for their response while my brain is whispering suggestions about what caused the grunts. *Nyoka hit them—Rucker, the giggler, and bird brain— with some kind of magic, likely invasive . . . mind control magic?*

"You may go, Alaster," Nyoka says with what sounds like a grin of satisfaction.

Foot stomps suggest Alaster—Ruck—left the area, which also suggests that there's at least one other access tunnel. That leaves at minimum four Spellbinders in the room. The odds seem good with our six to their four. Plus, we have the element of surprise on our hands. If we capture Kyson and Nyoka but the other two escape, so be it. We can find them later. Kyson and Nyoka are the biggest threats.

Belamey drops his masking and puts his hand up, giving a bladed wave forward. He remasks. Had I been closer to the front, I might have noticed the room wards designed to keep surprise visits from happening; we're visible the moment we cross into the room. Regardless, Kyson and Nyoka are stunned by our appearance.

My first glimpse of Nyoka is shocking. In my fleeting look at her, I see a Spellbinder with a light camo-grey do-rag around her head. She has a head necklace overtop, its V-shaped end draped over her forehead. A feather cape over a frilly high-collar shirt and wide-legged pants completes her ensemble. She isn't an imposing figure.

I have no time to study her further because the other two Spellbinders in Nyoka and Kyson's group waste no time attacking us. They strike without pause or care for their safety. It's such a vicious attack that it's probable Nyoka controlled and enhanced these Spellbinders, which explains the grunting noises from moments before. They're so strong that Belamey and Mayhem are working together to neutralize one Spellbinder while Griffin and I are working on the other one.

They aren't Spellbinders that I'm familiar with. What I am sure of is that they weren't the ones who captured Cian because the crow is Blake, and the cinereous vulture is Ruck. The marabou stork was the Fog, and the blue-footed booby was Wimpy. A chill travels over me as I think about how easily Nyoka and Kyson dismiss the lives and safety of their followers.

Kyson and Nyoka recover fast, and no magical attack hits them before they have shields in place. I'm aware of Fin and Brynlee moving forward as a team toward Kyson and Nyoka. I can't get a break in my own fight to do anything about them. These two Spellbinders controlled by Nyoka are fighting to kill us. We're in a fight for our lives. Magic flares, orbs crash, and yelling voices mingle in a room now filled with the stench of sweat and panic. *We're going to have to kill them. We can't expect to overcome them and then maintain control of them when their magical enhancement is so powerful. That would leave us vulnerable and too exhausted to protect ourselves or capture Kyson and Nyoka.*

I can't bring myself to form a death orb. That we're locked in this battle tells me my team can't bring themselves to commit murder either. My peripheral vision allows me to spot the protective dome Brynlee has over her and Fin, which is holding so far. Fin is throwing knives, but they're bouncing off the dome Kyson has over him and Nyoka.

The Spellbinder Griffin and I are fighting is tiring. The brief lull in his speed allows my paralytic orb to hit him, and Griffin moves in with the cuffs. There's no time for me to marvel about how elastic bands linked to a tiny metal jump ring can control a Spellbinder. I'm moving toward Brynlee and Fin when Kyson sneers at me. All the fine hairs on my body rise, and my adrenalin spikes.

Kyson lets the dome drop and shoves Nyoka at Fin, who had just released a knife laced with immobilizing magic. Nyoka didn't stand a chance; it was a double-crossing move she hadn't expected. I imagine she had weighed her worth to Kyson higher than it actually was.

Stumbling and trying to right her balance, the knife knicks the flesh of her outstretched hands. A small cut is all the immobilizing magic needs. The noise Nyoka makes is a cross between a scream and a sound of surprise. She drops to the floor, unable to move or access her magic.

Kyson uses that moment to throw two death orbs in our general direction—not aiming is an out-of-character act for him, and I wonder if I'm missing something. He grabs Brynlee, dropping a net like the one used to capture Cian over her. I don't know if Brynlee was his target all along, or if she became his target because she was closest to him. The latter seems the most likely answer. The net forces a shift, and Brynlee becomes her owl.

Kyson, eyes still on me, drops a smoke orb and escapes with my cousin in tow.

Chapter 16

The pounding of my pulse in my ears is like a drum corps with my voice screaming along. "I'll kill you!" My hands clenched into fists, I barrel toward the remaining smoke—which is blocking the exit tunnel—still bellowing my rage.

A hard body knocks into me from the side, and powerful arms clamp down on me in a bear hug that lifts my feet from the floor. I thrash my head around, trying to make contact with my captor. "Put me down!" I thunder, spit building in the corners of my mouth. Reaching for my magic, I discover I can't access it—it's bound tight.

I stop flailing and hang useless from Belamey's grip. The blended scent of earth, cardamom, cedar, and lavender, with undertones of cinnamon and vanilla wafting into my nasal passage, is what informs me I'm in Belamey's grip. Between my anger and adrenaline, the headiness that normally overcomes me from being close to Belamey is absent. A bone-deep tiredness fills me, and I can't keep from shaking.

Mayhem moves closer to the smoke lingering from Kyson's escape. *Strange that it hasn't evaporated.* She launches an orb of light into it. The orb hisses and melts. She pulls back from the smoke, which is now fading. "Poison," the shock in her voice is evident.

Belamey sucks in a deep breath of my hair. "We need to go. There has to be an exit down the tunnel Ruck and Kyson took."

Mayhem uses an air orb to clear away any lingering poison. Fin comes up beside Belamey and me and places the backside of her hand on my cheek. She gives a sad smile and strides after Mayhem, knives in hand.

"Grif?" Belamey says. I can hear movement coming up behind us. "You got that one?"

Nyoka comes into view. Griffin is pushing her forward. He has her braced with magic and is moving her legs with magic as well; the effects from the magic-coated knife haven't worn off her yet. Griffin stops so he can stand alongside Belamey.

Nyoka has to be about seventy-eight years old, but her skin—although pale—is flawless. Signs of aging are visible under her eyes and around her mouth, but they're noticeable only because I'm searching for them. Her subtle blue eyes fix on me as Griffin continues to usher her past. They seem to glow, with a rich blue outlining the iris.

"Yeah," Griffin says, but I don't hear anything else.

My blood is a loud rush in my ears. The sight of Nyoka makes my blood boil. I strain my muscles against Belamey. My hands are opening and closing at my sides, and I imagine tightening them around that woman's neck. I reach for my magic, using my anger to try to break the hold Belamey has placed on it. I'm unsuccessful.

Griffin bobs his head at me as he addresses Belamey. I hear him, but his voice sounds distant. "You going to put her down?"

I feel Belamey shake his head. "Not yet. She's not ready to play nice. You go in front of us with Nyoka. That way, we have her boxed in. Just in case."

Griffin doesn't respond. He nudges Nyoka, who stumbles but starts forward in a stilted step, a sign the immobilization magic is still wearing off. Belamey waits a few seconds before he follows, carrying me with him.

His husky voice is low as he speaks with his lips near my ear. "Out of the tunnels and home first. We need to figure out what to do with Nyoka. Maybe we can get her to tell us something." His voice cracks when he adds, "We'll get Brynlee back."

"We've gotten them all back so far, haven't we?" I hiss. "Just not alive." I feel ashamed of the anger oozing out of me.

Belamey has no more words. We plod along with me hanging limp in his arms, which have to tire at some point. There's the hum of chatter and moving feet, which I focus on like white noise. This tunnel is identical to the one we followed into the room, except the small torches lining the walls give off a pale light.

There's no fear of a fire because there's nothing to burn.

"You ready to walk on your own, Firecracker?"

I purse my lips and lower my eyes, even though Belamey can't see my face. "Yeah." He takes his time letting my feet reach the ground, but the motion snaps my brain out of the fog it's been in. "The other two Spellbinders?"

He lowers my feet the rest of the way to the ground and lets me go. "Kyson's death orbs killed them. Hard to say if they knew too much or if Kyson needed an easy, murderous fix. They were both in cuffs." His tone lightens. "So we're clear, Firecracker, your magic is still bound." I spin on him, and he raises his hands in the air. "Just for a little longer." I don't have the energy to do more than glare my displeasure at him.

"Found an exit up to ground level," Fin's voice drifts our way.

I roll my eyes at Belamey and stomp in Fin's direction. I find her standing at the base of a ladder, staring up. When I glance up, the bottom of a round wood plank is being hoisted higher. On the ladder, climbing in tandem with the plank, is Griffin.

"Nyoka is on the board," Fin says, lowering her eyes to me. I stare at her in confusion. "It's person-sized and new. Kind of ironic that she's using her method for moving victims."

I survey the ladder. "Ladder appears sturdy. You going up?"

Without warning, Fin clasps me to her in a hug. I return the embrace. "It wasn't supposed to be Brynlee," I mumble.

Fin's hands are rubbing my back, and she's still holding me tight. "Yes, but we added new people into the mix and . . ." her voice trails off.

I push away from her. "What?"

Her voice is lower than a whisper, and I strain to hear. "It's a successful way for him to maximize the pain he inflicts." She swallows.

I bow my head and close my eyes, fighting tears and anger. Fin pats my shoulder, and I hear her start her climb. I blow out a breath of air, trying to release tension, but it's hopeless. I'm aware that Belamey is standing near, respecting my space and need for silence.

"Thank you," I whisper to him as I regulate my breathing with deep belly breaths to engage my parasympathetic nervous system. *Don't cry.* I peek at him, and he closes his eyes and nods, his expression pained.

I move toward the ladder and head up, hoping there's a way to get back to the apartment as a group without putting much thought into a method of travel. As I clamber out of the well, I notice Fin has a driver and vehicle from her car lot here. She must've been able to get cell service while we were walking in the last section of the tunnel and made a call, instructing them to track her phone to find us. We aren't far from the prison grounds. The other tunnel that led away from the ladder must go under the jail.

I wait for Belamey and help him cover the well. No secretary bird here. Rye told me the first time we used a well to enter the tunnels that there weren't many well entrances left, but that the remaining ones were all guarded by secretaries. I wonder if this was Ophelia's well at one point, or did Kyson and Nyoka kill another innocent Spellbinder who didn't agree with their plans? Belamey opens the door for the front passenger seat and ushers me in, trying to keep a distance between me and Nyoka. I don't feel like killing her anymore—hurting her maybe, but not taking her life. Either way, I don't argue. I get in.

Our driver is a young man, college-age—probably a part-time employee at Fin's lot that she trusts will mind his own business and not ask questions. He doesn't take his eyes off the spot in front of him. I hear Belamey climb in the back and slam his door.

"That's it, Kevin. Drive, please. My apartment," Fin says from the rear. I close my eyes and wait for the drive to end.

When we arrive, Belamey's cell phone is on the breakfast bar, forgotten or left on purpose, ringing. He crosses the room in a few strides and picks it up. "Yeah?" he says and pauses. "Wait." He puts the phone on speaker and sets it on the counter. We're all in the room now.

Rye's voice speaks. "It's done. An earth dweller was waiting for us, an old friend named Alefall. She went with Pearle. So, I didn't go inside the Allurist Detention Centre, but I waited until I was sure Pearle was successful."

I can't process how I feel about the news that Grama Pearle is locked inside a prison that's sunken away from the world. I feel numb. It's like Rye is reading my thoughts. "Kori, Alefall assured us they'll bring the detention centre out of the stone when it's safe again. She gave me a method of communication."

"We have Nyoka," Belamey says.

"Kyson got away," Fin yells. We all gape at her, unsure why she's being so loud.

"Hold Nyoka," Rye says. "I'm on my way." The line cuts out, and when we can hear Rye's voice again, she says, "Alefall also provided me with a travel method and a guide to help me. The travel system is built into the rock, so sometimes we get pretty deep, but it's kind of like a bullet train. We surfaced to call you. Anyway, we'll be there soon." The phone disconnects.

"That reminds me," Fin mumbles to herself. She turns and hurries into her bedroom. The door closes and reopens almost instantly. She scurries into the kitchen, grabs the coffee pot we left brewing and half full, a bag of chips, and heads back to her room. The whole time, she's mumbling about the Influencer symbol.

I scan everyone in the room to see if they know what Fin is going on about, but when my eyes land on Nyoka, I forget about Fin. My eyes narrow, and my nostrils flare. "We need to find out what she knows."

I squint and bend in Nyoka's direction. She's slack-jawed, unmoving. The rise and fall of her chest are too slow and restricted to be normal. Her eyes are open, but there's a grey fog swirling in them. "What in the blazing hell is wrong with her?"

Griffin muscles Nyoka toward the breakfast bar and pushes her into a sitting position on the floor. It doesn't take much effort since she's zombie-ish.

"She's put herself into . . ." Mayhem snaps her fingers as she struggles for the word.

"Suspended animation," Belamey spits.

I fight the urge to move closer and nudge Nyoka with my foot. "What?"

"Think hypnosis or trance," Mayhem says, kicking Nyoka's thigh. The kick doesn't elicit a response. "She isn't going to respond to external stimuli, and she can't communicate. She's unconscious, with very low body functioning."

"So, she's useless to us?" I can't keep the frustration from making my voice high-pitched. "Can't we snap her out of it?"

"Nope." Griffin sighs, then stands and moves away from her. He fiddles with the buckle on his belt, the one that's now paired with the elastic cuffs that control Nyoka's magic and keep her within a short distance of him.

"The cuffs don't control suspended animation?" I huff.

"Although suspended animation is specific to Spellbinders, there isn't magic involved. It's a skill that can be learned, practised, and improved until a person becomes a master at it. Nyoka has had decades to perfect her ability in prison," Mayhem explains.

I cross my arms over my chest, and my foot taps the floor. Watching Nyoka, my brain lurches through devious ideas for trying to get someone talking—things that I'm sure would make Kyson and Nyoka proud: melting flesh with hot water, cigarette burns, pulling fingernails . . .

Belamey moves up close and slides his arm across my shoulder. I lean my head sideways against him, and we stand there in silence, staring at Nyoka.

Chapter 17

Rye arrives deep in the night, but nobody is sleeping when she comes in. She isn't alone. If her company surprises anybody, they hide their shock well. Even I school my features. She enters through the front door with a three-foot-tall earth dweller. Its fog-grey skin keeps me from thinking she's brought a child home with her. Earth dweller skin has an extraordinary smoothness, giving them a youthful appearance even when they are hundreds of years old.

Belamey greets Rye with a hug and then bows to the earth dweller that Rye introduces as Dwalin. Dwalin makes an exaggerated bow that causes his many long braids to drop forward in front of him. He stands, flicking them behind him. "I'm here to help with the tomfools wrangling you." His voice is resonant.

Fin comes out of her bedroom, where she has been

working on something unknown. All she says about her work is that it requires "great imagination," which echoes what she told me Grama Pearle said to her. My takeaway is that Fin is busy in connection with Grama Pearle's mysterious gift to her. This time, while she was working, Fin left her door open. So, she heard Rye and the earth dweller arrive and came out in response to Dwalin's comment. "We need a lot of help with that, Master Dwalin," Fin says.

Mayhem observes the exchanges in silence. Arms crossed, she sits on the kitchen counter across from the breakfast bar. She isn't being rude; she's just the type of person who watches and interacts only when necessary. Dwalin and Rye take Mayhem's overwatch from the counter in stride as we fill them in on everything that has occurred.

Rye's face is a mask that doesn't provide any clues to her thoughts or feelings. It's what I've come to expect from her; I've learned that she *is* feeling and thinking, but her life has taught her that thoughts and emotions are for her alone—sharing them could be deadly. So, I don't take offence at what could be perceived as cold detachment.

"We don't have time to keep standing around," I say with more force than I meant. "Kyson will kill Brynlee." I crack my neck to the left and then the right, trying to ease my discomfort.

Rye considers Nyoka. She shakes her head. "Suspended animation. Cunning."

Tapping on the living room window interrupts our conversation. I'm the first to enter the room. A crow is on the sill outside, rapping the glass with its beak. Beside it, on the ledge, is a small rectangular box. Cold fingers of dread dance across my flesh. Satisfied that I've seen him and the package, the crow squawks and flies off.

I run through the living room and yank the window open. "Blake!" I scream into the night, but he's gone. Standing staring down at an inch-wide box that's about three inches long, I can't bring myself to pick it up.

"I'll get it, Kori," Fin whispers next to me. She reaches past me, careful not to bump into me, and picks it up before she moves toward the kitchen where the coffeemaker is sputtering. The bitter, roasted-nut smell is just starting to be fragrant.

The heat of Belamey's body presses against me from behind as he reaches around and closes the window. His hands close on my shoulders, and he steers me away. We enter the kitchen at a snail's pace.

The box is on the breakfast bar, open. Everyone is staring at it. Even Mayhem has come down from her perch on the counter, although she looks as if she's second-guessing that decision. She keeps glancing at the window and door like she's considering leaving. Then there is Fin; she's resting against Griffin with an expression of horror plastered on her face. *It can't be good.* My flesh feels like it's crawling, and I'm having trouble swallowing.

Rye doesn't turn to view us. She just senses that we have entered the room. "You might want to stay over there, Kori."

Pulling out of Belamey's grip, I cross the room. I grab

the edge of the breakfast bar to steady the wave of dizziness that overcomes me. I blink at the box's contents. My hand moves, but I pull back before my fingers even graze the surface. There are two things inside. A severed finger, nail painted a midnight blue—Brynlee's favourite colour. Alongside it is a folded piece of paper.

I've seen my share of unpleasant things. A career as a police officer can be riddled with experiences that are outside what a regular person is expected to encounter. But having a distressing experience that involves my living space, my family, and my personal life doesn't allow for the detachment I mastered as a cop. I feel defenceless as I stare at this severed piece of my cousin's body. A body part that was delivered to my home as a message to me and my friends. Bile rises in my throat, burning and sour. I clench my jaw and swallow multiple times.

"We didn't open the paper yet," Fin's words are slow and overly pronounced. "Kyson uses that magic technique of sinking his voice into paper to speak a message once opened so . . ."

I clear my throat and move my hand toward the box, but I freeze partway. Belamey's hand closes over mine. "I'll get the paper."

I nod. My voice sounds distant when I speak. "There are threads of magic, but they're word strands."

Belamey reaches in and plucks the paper out. He wastes no time unfolding it. A maniacal laugh vibrates out of the paper that Belamey has dropped on the counter. My jaw tightens, making my back teeth ache and my hands ball up so tight that I can feel my nails puncturing my palms. The laughter abruptly cuts off, unsettling me.

In the pause, I imagine him composing himself. Then Kyson's hateful voice fills the air. "Kori Ember, you'll meet me. If you don't come, I will send you pieces of Brynlee Greyson until either you arrive or there is nothing left of her." He snickers. "If anyone else comes, or someone comes with you, I will kill them *and* Brynlee." His voice takes on a smugness. "A second message has been left for you with the location of our meeting."

I run back to the living room window. An identical box is on the ledge outside. I yank the window up, anger pumping through my veins. I embrace my anger as the support method that's available to me at the moment. Other supports are present, but right now, anger will protect me from my other emotions, the ones I can't process quickly and don't want to deal with. I will make time for them when Brynlee is safe and we've captured Kyson. There's no crow or any other bird in sight. I snatch the box and slam the window. Everyone from the kitchen is huddled in the living room entranceway.

"You want me to open it, Kori?" Fin's eyes are wide, and she's grimacing.

I pull the lid off the box, bracing to find another finger with a note. The note is tucked under a long midnight blue fingernail. I gag and drop the box. Fin is with me in a second, arms around me. Horrified, I bury my head in her shoulder and fight the sobs; I feel guilty because I can't control them. I can't watch who picks up the note and opens it, but I hear Kyson's voice. "Meet me at the old jail. Come in the same door as the last time. Come alone. The sooner, the better."

I suck a deep breath and push away from Fin. I surprise myself with the steady, low pitch of my voice. My anger is sharp and focused. In a split second, I make my decision. "I'm going now."

The energy in the room is supercharged. Rye's voice dominates it. "No, you're not."

Part of me realizes that I have become the person driven by emotion and impulse; I understand Rye's actions while there was still a chance to save Cian differently now that Kyson took Brynlee. It's not that I didn't want to save Cian, but our relationship was different and I wasn't as clouded by intimate emotion. I'm about to argue, but Rye's countenance terrifies me. Experiencing anything but an emotionless mask on her features is unexpected.

"I'll go," she says. "I'm not going to list the reasons this is a good choice. Giving Kyson Adelgrief what he wants is a bad idea." She points a finger at Belamey. "Don't." Her expression has the same effect on him as it has on me.

Griffin's voice draws Rye's unguarded countenance. "At least let me come with you, Rye." His hands move to his buckle, presumably to pass it off to one of us, but they fall away as he interprets Rye's posture.

Her face becomes soft with gratitude. "I can't risk losing anybody else I love," she says so softly that I struggle to make out her words. "Nobody else can do what I do," she says as her appearance alters. I'm blinking idiotically at Rye, who now resembles a replica of me. She doesn't underestimate Belamey or my stubborn determination. She uses our surprise against us, and we find ourselves trapped under a dissipating dome. The only person outside of it is Rye.

Griffin's hands fly to his buckle. Rye wouldn't be so reckless as to let the binding between Nyoka and the buckle sever. His hands relax, confirming my assumption—the connection is intact.

Belamey's voice shakes when he cries out, "Mother!"

I can't place how I feel. Too many reactions are shifting inside me; waves of apprehension, dread, guilt, panic, sadness, shock, anger, and helplessness crash against me and recede to be replaced by the next warring emotion. I struggle to form a response. My hands shake when I bring them up to rub my temples.

I'm hyper-focused on Rye as she changes into her form as Rye. She makes a kiss and blows it to Belamey. She walks from the room without a backward glance, and we hear the kitchen door close. We can't see her, but I imagine she left the apartment on foot disguised as me. She can't shift into her bird when she's supposed to be me and she can't assume the form of my hummingbird. So, flying isn't an option. We don't know if the apartment is being watched.

Dwalin's voice rumbles under the dome. "She's an amazing Spellbinder. Such an honour to be considered her friend."

"We think so, too," Fin says.

Mayhem is so quiet that it's easy to forget about her, especially with everything that has just happened. I glance in her direction. She's standing with her head down and her arms wrapped around herself. I step closer to her but respect her personal space. Keeping my voice low, I call her name. "Mayhem." She looks up at me but remains in her closed-off stance. "Are you okay?"

She stares at me for a moment, like she can't comprehend my words, before she shakes herself. Her arms drop to her sides and she steels her spine. "Yeah. It's just . . ." her eyes swing toward Belamey and then back to me. "I felt like I lost Blake a long time ago. Kyson became his world." She shrugs. "I'm used to things in my life coming and going. They go more often than not. But Brynlee . . ."

Belamey drops his arm over Mayhem's shoulders and pulls her close to his side, a comfort she allows.

Silence falls over us. None of us looking at each other. We have to wait for the dome to fade before we can do anything. There's no way to tell how fast it'll dissolve, but knowing Rye, it won't be fast. There's nothing to be said, and talking will heighten our hopeless situation.

My mind is cycling through our losses. Decisions I've made and decisions we've made as a group. *Could we have done anything different?* I slouch to the floor. Belamey, unable to stand still, is now pacing like a caged animal, his feet crossing the path of my view. I count the times he paces by, trying to distract my spiralling thoughts—time is dragging.

Chapter 18

The dome quivers, lending a sphere-shaped, shimmering appearance to the air. There's a sputtering followed by a feeble hiss, and the dome is gone. The air outside the dome stinks of stale coffee.

It's been hours since Rye left, long enough that she should've returned. Belamey stalks to the window and throws it open. There's so much power in his step that I half expect him to dive out the window in human form and shift in the air, but he hasn't lost all sense of control. He pauses in front of the open window and glances at me before he transforms and flies off.

"We got this," I say to Griffin, Fin, and Dwalin. I look at Mayhem. She's sleeping in a sitting position, leaning back against the wall. "Stay here in case Rye returns or there's an attack." I shift, giving thanks to my speedy hummingbird wings, and steer toward the old jail. I fly straight to the prison door and transform.

Belamey prowls through the open gate with me on his heels. I can tell by the feeling in the air that there's nobody here, at least in the sense of a person who is holding life. I follow Belamey anyway, driven by the same urge to be sure we're alone. "There're no strands of magic anywhere," I say. *It makes little sense. Unless . . . of course, this was a trap all along.* "Where would Kyson go? Not to The Society of the Blood Wind house and not into the tunnels."

Belamey spins on me, his eyes wide. His muscles clench, and the veins in his neck pop. My adrenalin is so high my vision is spotty, and the overwhelming sense of dread that hits me makes me gasp. *No, no, no, no. The apartment.*

We're both running full speed back the way we came. The movement of our feet blends with the thunder of my pulse in my ears. Belamey shifts mid-stride as we breech the gate; his wings take over the powerful movement that his legs had moments before.

It's a bit disorientating to transform this way. As the pressure squeezes my body and my wings take my weight, my brain processes more slowly, not realizing right away that the footfall it's anticipating isn't coming. My bird body wavers on the air currents, and then I'm in control and flying home at full speed.

The window is open as I zoom in, shifting, my feet skidding across the floor. My eyes surveying as I try to master my actions. Everyone is here, and nobody is hurt. Neither Rye nor Brynlee have returned. Relief wars with disappointment. *Now, where do we go? We need to find his base of operation.*

I hear a light tap and turn my head toward the sound. Something white is cascading down the wall near the entrance to the kitchen. It's a paper airplane, I realize. It must have come in the open living room window. I'm closest, so after a fast inspection for magic, I pick it up. *Please don't let this be a message saying they're dead.* I swallow the lump forming in my throat and unfold the plane.

As anticipated, Kyson's voice rasps out of the paper. The level of anger in his words makes me bend the top half of my body backwards, trying to put distance between my head and my hand, which is still holding the paper. "I know about the Allurist Detention Centre." There's breathing before he continues. "I already have what I needed from there." More breathing.

"What does that mean?" There is panic in Fin's voice. "Did he help more lunatic Spellbinders esca—" Screams coming out of the paper cut off the rest of Fin's words. Her hands fly to her ears, and she reverses up against Griffin.

My knees give way. The paper falls from my hand to the floor, but the screaming continues. I can't bring myself to look at Belamey. I'm staring at the paper. It resembles a regular piece of printer paper, blank with folded lines. The screams fade to whimpers. In the whimpering, Rye's voice is whispering what I first interpret as nonsense. But as she repeats it, it sounds like, "Fin, bring it."

I lift my eyes without lifting my head and note Fin's mouth moving, forming silent words. My lip-reading skills aren't top-notch, and the angle I'm in isn't doing me any favours, but I swear she's mouthing, "I will bring it!"

Kyson's message isn't over. "I'm going to take my time with them." If it's possible to hear a sneer, then it's happening with these words. "You locked away someone important of mine, so I'll return the favour." The paper bursts into flame, odourless, and turns to ash.

Dwalin is in front of me. I straighten on my knees so we are eye to eye. "You need to follow him," he rumbles, pointing over his shoulder.

I'm not sure what *him* he's talking about, but it's apparent when I look up that Belamey has left the apartment. Griffin comes out of the kitchen and is at the window in a few strides. I hadn't seen him go to the kitchen. *How long was I fixated on the ashes on the floor?* Griffin shifts and goes after Belamey. Mayhem follows before we can stop her.

I'm clueless as to how much time there is between Belamey and Griffin leaving, given I don't know when Belamey left. *Fin.* I cast my eyes to her. *I can't leave her here alone.* Dwalin's nose presses against mine—cold and hard—and I jerk my head back, but he just moves closer. At this proximity, I'm aware of the root vegetable smell that clings to this earth dweller. It isn't unpleasant, but it isn't what my olfactory senses expected.

"I will stay with Fin. She and I will be safe," Dwalin booms. There's no doubt in my mind that he means it. Whether he can stand by it, I'm not sure, but I have to make a choice, and fast. I scootch my whole body away from Dwalin and study Fin. She's nodding and holding her knives.

I hurry into the kitchen. Nyoka has been put under a holding dome, still in suspended animation. The dome's thread suggests that it won't dissipate, but we can release Nyoka if we need to. She's fine where she is for now.

I run to the living room. "Thank you," I call as I race toward the window and dive out, not giving any thought to what would happen if I couldn't shift. I transform, though, and head toward The Society of the Blood Wind house because I know without a doubt that's where Belamey is going to check for clues about his mother. It's a desperate move but the only logical one at our disposal.

As soon as I transform into my human form on the sidewalk in front of The Society of the Blood Wind house, Griffin's arms lock around me. "The wards weren't reset, Kori. It should've been a warning to him, but he was so focused on Rye. Reckless, he didn't even stop to think, and I wasn't close enough to stop him."

I see Belamey through the front window. It's a brief glimpse. He steps away from the window and into the depths of the house. *He lost his mother once. I can't imagine the pain. And now the possibility of losing her again . . .*

I can't be sure if he's injured, but he doesn't appear to be as The Society of the Blood Wind house closes like a tomb. Stone without creases encases the house, sealing Belamey away and giving Kyson's recent message a whole new meaning. A dark magic clings to every surface of the encasement.

Griffin hasn't blocked my magic; I can feel it humming in my body. His low, rough voice penetrates the fog my brain is in—my single-minded narrowness to get to Belamey. "We can't help him right now."

I scream, loud and long. I can feel the veins of my neck bulging with the force of my voice tearing past them. My hands have grabbed onto Griffin's arms where they're holding me, and I'm squeezing as hard as I can. If it hurts him, he's taking it without sound or action. I know I'm not in control of myself, but I can't get a handle on it. I need to let this out.

My throat feels raw. I pry my hands off of Griffin. With hesitation, he releases me. I close my eyes and roll my neck. The breath of air I pull in is jagged. "How do we . . . is he . . ." When I open my eyes, I lock them on Griffin.

"We need Kyson," he says.

"Mayhem! Where is she? She followed you and Belamey?"

Griffin points to the tree. A black crow—Mayhem—is sitting on a branch, staring at us. I release the air I was holding. It's a small win that she wasn't trapped in the house as well. I turn left and right, scanning up and down the street. I'm searching, although I don't know for what. *Is Kyson brazen enough to be close by, watching?* The street is empty. After all of my screaming and whatever display we might've put on with all this, not a soul has come to investigate. *How does a normie's conditioning stay intact through all of this?*

"Griffin?" I point up the sidewalk.

A little girl appears. Spellbinder or normie, I can't be sure. There's no magic clinging to her, but if I were guessing, she's about five years old, so perhaps she's still too young to be showing threads or even using magic. She's skipping and staring right at us. Her hands are swinging with the flow of her movements. Her right hand is holding a tube. We wait in silence, watching her. As she gets closer, the playfulness of her humming reaches us, and she stops skipping and walks up to us.

She considers Griffin first but walks up to me instead. She smiles. "He said to give this to you." She holds up the tube.

It was smart of Kyson to use a child to deliver his next message. The stakes have risen. Had he sent Blake or another of his minions, the likelihood of us catching him and extracting information would have been too high. I'm stiff and have to force my rigid muscles to move. When I take the tube from her hand with a murmured thanks, she shrugs and skips away.

My pointer finger is tapping against the side of the tube, my pent-up frustration visible with the action. I'd like to slam a door or pound my fist on a tabletop, but I'm standing on a sidewalk. Short of stomping my feet and screaming some more, my options are limited. I sigh. The tube doesn't weigh much. The paper it's made from is rough, like the pulpy fibres weren't blended in and hardened as bumps on the surface.

"Not here, Kori," Griffin says.

I give a snort of impatience. "Okay." I gaze reluctantly

at the house. My stomach is a knot. "Home."

The crow squawks and flies away. Griffin nods but waits for me to transform and start flying toward the apartment before he shifts and follows.

When I shift in the living room, I see Fin and Dwalin standing with their backs against the wall, in a fight stance, their eyes locked on the window. "Good job, guys," I say, to disarm their defensive posture. "Where's Mayhem?"

"A crow flew by the window a few minutes before you came in," Fin says. "There," she points to the window as Mayhem swoops in and Griffin is right behind her. They transform.

Fin is watching the window. "Where is Belamey?"

My arms hang at my sides and I step backward like I'm trying to get space from Fin's question and the answer. I can't bring myself to explain. I implore Griffin with my eyes.

"Trapped in The Society of the Blood Wind house," he says. "Alive for now, but trapped."

Fin makes a strangled sound and rushes to me. She catches sight of the tube in my hand and stops. "What's that?" she asks.

"Not sure yet," I mumble. I pull the end of the tube off as I walk toward the breakfast bar. I have a pretty good idea of what might be in the tube, and I don't want to dump it out on my hand. Bracing myself, I upend the tube on the counter, and sure enough, a midnight blue fingernail comes out. I'm thankful that it landed with the polished side up, so the more graphic indications that it was pulled from a nail bed aren't visible. I don't gag this time, but I blanch. Mayhem keeps her distance, her face wiped of emotion.

"At least it's a nail and not a full finger," Fin says weakly.

I bang the tube on the counter to make sure there isn't anything else. A puff of ash comes out, and Kyson's voice follows. "Do you remember what I told you all? I promised that our time would come, and with it, each of your deaths."

I hear his words, but they aren't my focus. Concentrating on his words hasn't been helpful; I can't imagine it will be any different this time. We need to get an idea of where he might be. I'm listening to what I hear in the background. The crackle of fire and strange noises feel uncomfortable and mildly familiar.

My eyes are wide. "He's at a crematorium!"

Chapter 19

Fin rams a cup of coffee into my hand. It's a hot, solid weight. The scent and mist rising from the liquid give me a small energy boost. "Coffee, Dwalin?" Fin asks, stuffing a mug into Mayhem's waiting hand.

"Indeed, we earth dwellers love the fruit of the coffea plant. We eat them, drink them, and cook with them."

Fin passes him a coffee mug filled just below the rim. The twelve-ounce cup is oversized in his hands. "This is the biggest mug you have?"

Her shoulders pull up to her ears. "Sorry."

Dwalin upends his mug and downs all the liquid. My coffee is hot and bitter as I take a mouthful. *How did he not melt the inside of his mouth?* I dismiss Dwalin's coffee drinking, and other thoughts roll through my mind. They're clouded with blank patches. There's so much we don't know and haven't known the whole time. There have been so many fatal errors that we can't afford to bumble into something again. None of our successful missions matter. One hit at us in places close to home, and we let emotion muddy all our actions. I look at Fin. She is leaning on the counter across from the breakfast bar, Griffin alongside her. Both are sipping coffees.

"What about that, bwitch?" Fin asks, pointing her toes at the semi-conscious Nyoka. Fin has a smirk on her face for using her favourite word combo of witch and bitch.

"Suspended animation slows all body functions. She won't need sustenance for days, if not longer," Mayhem explains. I note that Mayhem seems to be recovering a bit from the shock over Blake's corruption and Brynlee's capture and mutilation.

Fin shrugs. "Well, we better get to it." I'm surprised by the hint of tiredness that she allows to enter her voice. "He can't be at the local crematorium. Agreed?"

I speak into my coffee cup. "Yeap, but he also can't be that far."

"The Society of the Blood Wind has their own crematorium," Griffin advises. "It isn't a well-known fact. I learned of it several years ago, but it never came up in conversation or concerning our missions." He pushes his shoulders down and moves his neck like he's trying to ease out discomfort. "Let's just say that Dolion had some hobbies that are best left unspoken," he says. "Not to get into the details, but a personal crematorium was involved on occasion."

My hands are raking through my hair. "Okay, so

where is it?"

"Deep in The Society of the Blood Wind's backyard."

Fin's voice is shrill. "How? We've never seen it or heard anyone talking about it."

"I lived there, and I didn't even know," Mayhem adds.

Griffin chuckles. "It's underground."

"Tunnels?" Fin whispers, squirming around at the thought.

"No."

"So, there's an above-ground entrance that doesn't involve the tunnels?" I realize my tone is more intrigued by this than it should be.

"There's a shed that houses the stairs down to the crematorium. The venting systems are all in the same area. It's set up to mimic a shed with a wood stove inside so it's less likely to draw attention. The odours might create questions, but anyone hanging out at the house knows better than to ask or talk about certain things."

None of us speak, each considering what we've just learned. We leave the question of how to get inside unsaid. We could just walk across the property and march into the shed, but it's not in our best interest or the interest of the people we are trying to save. The shed is likely guarded or warded, maybe both. Plus, having the element of surprise on our side wouldn't be bad for us.

Dwalin is the first to speak. "Do you trust me?"

I'm not sure what to say. Do we trust an earth dweller we just met and know nothing about? Hell no is the answer that comes to mind. Instead of blurting it out, I assess the creature. He's standing with his feet spread and spine straight. He isn't trying to make himself look taller; he's just a proud life form.

"Hell yes," Fin says, not muting her volume or tone. She shoots me a glare that says I was taking too long to provide my answer.

"Very good." He gives a strong nod. "Rye showed me where The Society of the Blood Wind house is. I need to go there now and check on something. If all goes well, I can get us in without using the tunnels or the shed." He eyes each one of us. "Wait for me. I will be an hour." He marches through the kitchen and out the door.

Our mood is heavy. We've been in tight spots before, but this—capturing and killing our loved ones—is personal and profoundly impactful. Kyson's ability to disregard all boundaries and kill without compunction puts him at an advantage that we'll never be able to compete with or understand. I'm fidgeting and twitching, restless. I run my hands through my hair and puff out my cheeks. *Can I cross the lines that Kyson ignores? Can I kill just to kill? Would I end all of this if I. . .* I blow my air out and open my mouth to speak my thoughts, but I don't get a chance.

Fin has turned to face Griffin. She's pressed up against him with her lower back arched away so she can watch his face. "Marry me?"

My jaw drops, then I use my hand to push my jaw closed. I'm staring at them with eyes so wide there's a pressure setting off warning signals in my brain that I'm going to pop my eyeballs right out of my skull. Griffin chuckles. "I thought you'd never ask." His arms circle her and pull her in for a kiss that makes me blush.

Fin pulls away, vibrating with excitement. She turns, smiling like an idiot. "I'm getting married!" She sashays close enough to grab me and spins us. "You're my maid of honour, and don't you dare balk. Not ever, Kori."

"I wouldn't dream of it, Fin." And I genuinely mean it. "No balking." I smile at her. "Congratulations."

"And Mayhem, would you be a bridesmaid?"

Mayhem nods, and Fin hugs her. Fin gives a self-satisfied smile, blows Griffin a kiss, and hurries to her room.

Griffin and I stare at each other. I laugh despite everything. "Leave it to Fin to give us just what we needed. A smile and some happiness."

Griffin smiles. "She has a way of doing that." There's wonder in his voice as he stares in the direction she exited. "Excuse me." He moves toward the bedroom without looking at me.

"I'm going to get a shower," Mayhem says. Without a glance at me, she leaves the room.

I leer at Nyoka. It's just me and her in the room now. My thoughts darken, and my eyes dart to Fin's room and then back to Nyoka. My voice is choked with emotion. "I could kill you right now. And I should kill you. I want to kill you." My top teeth sink onto my bottom lip with a pressure that almost punctures it. I let out a moan and drop to my knees in front of her. I'm muttering unintelligible words to myself.

A death orb is in my hands, a response to the desperation of my thoughts and the feeling of hate that threatens to overwhelm me. Greenish-grey, it's fevered, pulsing with copper-coloured electricity. The energy humming through it vibrates up my arms. My whole body is trembling with the war inside me. *She doesn't deserve to live.* My eyes drift from Nyoka to my orb. *Who am I to decide that?*

With a dry mouth and a racing heartbeat, my head moves left and right. It's a slow movement that increases until my head is shaking no so quickly that my vision blurs. *This isn't who I am. I'm not a murderer.* I'm sweating. "Blazing hell," I swear. "Blazing hell," I repeat louder. "Blazing hell!" I yell, not caring if Fin or Griffin hear me.

The orb in my hand vanishes. I crumple over on my knees, my head on the floor and my hands cupped over my head. Sucking in a deep breath, I shove off the floor and stand. I glare down at the evil Spellbinder. My chin trembles, but my voice is monotone when I say, "Sorry that so much hatred marks your existence."

I move to the living room to pace and wait. Floating my chakra stones over my palm as I walk, I focus on them and ground myself in the moment. I don't hear the front door open, but since I'm confident in our wards, I don't think about it when I hear someone enter the kitchen. As I'm drawn out of my walking meditation, Dwalin announces, "I can get us in, my friends."

I walk with purposeful strides to the kitchen. Mayhem is sitting on the counter sipping a coffee. I have no idea how long she's been sitting there. I was so lost in my own thoughts that I didn't hear the shower start or stop. Griffin and Fin come out of the bedroom. We all spare a moment to ensure there's no change with Nyoka. There isn't. We turn our attentiveness to Dwalin. He opens his hands wide. "I can burrow us in."

"Like dig a tunnel as we are in it with you?" I ask.

"Yes. The very nature of who I am allows me to do this. And I'm fast." Dwalin judges each of our facial expressions. We're all displaying a semblance of shock and questioning. "You Spellbinder tomfools." I know tomfool is an insult, but Dwalin's tone is one of teasing amusement. "It's safe for me to do, and a bit of earth dweller magic is involved that allows the material I mine to become infused with the surrounding structure. Waste is limited, and the tunnel is reinforced as I dig."

It isn't like we have many other options. The thought of involving anybody else who could become a victim isn't something we're comfortable with. Kyson wants revenge on us. If we fall to him, those who aren't involved now can handle what happens after. Hopefully, it won't come to that.

I made my decision. This is happening. "Griffin?"

"Yeah."

I nod at Nyoka. "What about her?"

He touches the buckle. "Well, under different circumstances, she'd have to come because of the cuffs and buckle. But whatever Rye did with this dome has altered the distance the buckle and cuffs can go from each other. I tested my hunch about the dome and the cuffs when I followed Belamey to The Society of the Blood Wind house. Nyoka has no visible injuries, which means the buckle and cuffs can be far apart while she's under that dome."

I flinch because of the question I have, but I force the words out. "If Rye . . . if she dies . . ." I'm assuming she isn't already dead. "With her gone, what would happen?"

"The dome should stay intact until we trip it open, whether Rye is alive or not."

I'm not sure if that makes me feel any level of reassurance. I push away the notion that Rye could already be dead. There isn't room for those thoughts in my head. I turn to Dwalin. "Where do we start?"

Chapter 20

Dwalin leads us across the road and up the street, just past the Ember house. I cross my fingers that nobody notices us filing past because I can't stand the thought of endangering anybody else or explaining that Brynlee's been captured and we've only been successful in collecting parts of her. We pass unnoticed, and I take the small win when we cut down the side of someone's property about four houses away from the Ember house. I'm also happy that my family is taking Dodo's warning to hole up and stay safe seriously.

We're skirting along a row of cedar hedges that line the yard. The citrusy pine smell is strong but refreshing. I draw in a deep sniff, noting the soft tickle of the branches on my flesh as we creep past. The house is in darkness. They must be out on their day's errands. A normie family resides here, so they wouldn't be under lockdown like Spellbinders are. Even if they're like Fin, it's doubtful they would know what's going on in our magical lives—just because they can see doesn't mean they want to be involved. Dwalin stops in the far corner of the yard, where there's a visible hole that's hardly the diameter of a human body.

"I started this on my way to get you guys," he says, indicating the opening in the ground. "I figured that knowing right where we needed to start would save us time."

Dwalin moves toward the hole, stops, and turns to face us. We've gathered around his dig site, each of us with expressions of uncertainty. "I'm going to dive in, but that's because of how I need to dig this section of our tunnel. I want you to all enter feet first, please. It's a bit of a straight drop." He smiles.

"Keep your mouth closed on the way down. And you may even want to hold your breath for the drop." Dwalin turns and walks to the edge of the hole. "Give me three minutes before the first person follows, and then every three minutes after that until we're all in."

I consider us waiting above ground until the tunnelling is complete, but if Dwalin tunnels into the crematorium accidentally before we all meet up with him, then he could be in danger. It's best we stay together. "Dwalin, is a three-minute interval enough time? I don't want us landing on each other when we reach the bottom." I'm thinking about the drop from the ladder when we entered the tunnels to travel under the super jail; we got delayed moving away from the ladder because of the murk monster. With this scenario, I have no idea what to expect.

"Yes, I dig fast. Three minutes even gives me a cushion of time to stop and have a chat, if I wanted to, which I don't." With that, he bends and dives into the hole with his arms steepled over his head like he's getting into a pool.

Fin angles forward to gander in the hole. "Going into the tunnels under the town was creepy, but this puts that to shame."

Mayhem doesn't give in to curiosity at all. She settles herself cross-legged on the ground to wait. As much as I'm anxious and feel a whole gambit of other emotions coursing through me, interest is winning out. I crouch and bend my head to the hole, trying to hear. I glance at my watch and stand. "Should we conceal this area?"

Griffin puts a modest dome over us, blending us with the surrounding foliage. Anyone viewing the property would observe what it always looks like in this corner of the yard—a lawn without a hole. The dome will stay in place until dark falls.

"Three minutes," Fin says, rubbing her hands together. "Who's first?"

"Me." I sit on the grass and put my feet into the hole. "Griffin, this is going to be tight for you."

"I'll make it work."

I move my bottom to the edge and slide in. My arms go up over my head by default of how I entered. I can feel bits of soil crumbling off the wall as I fall, and I'm thankful for the tip about holding my breath and keeping my mouth closed. My eyes are shut, too. I feel like I'm falling for an impossible time frame, and then the ground rushes up under my feet. The impact knocks me backwards into the wall. It's rough and hard, not soil at all.

I open my eyes, but I'm in darkness. Suddenly, it's like I can't get air. My breaths are quick and shallow. *I'm going to die.* My body is heating up and I can feel moisture beading my forehead. I want to run, but I just dropped straight down a body-sized hole, so I have nowhere to go. *No, no, no.* My eyes dart in the darkness, to no avail.

"Dwalin," I squeak. Movement in front of me doesn't alleviate any of my panic. "Dwalin?"

"Don't panic, Kori."

The sound of Dwalin's voice is a reassurance, and I press my palm against my heart to let that comfort sink in.

The rustling movement has stopped and Dwalin speaks again. "You can light an orb, and you need to move closer while I dig so that nobody drops onto your head."

My light orb sparks up before Dwalin has even finished talking. I crowd him, pushing down the shaky laughter that is bubbling inside me—when panic becomes relief, it does strange things to the nervous system. He nods at me and spins toward the solid wall of rock in front of him. He's digging horizontally, making a walking tunnel for us. Glancing around, I note that the soil I was falling through at the beginning of my descent turned to rock at some point, which explains why my back feels scraped where it hit the wall. I don't think about how far down Dwalin has dug to reach solid stone or that I'm at his mercy to get to the surface.

Given that Dwalin is burrowing through the rock, I expect the air to be clogged with dust. But my nose doesn't detect any hint of grit when I inhale. The pale light from my orb doesn't have dust hanging in it, either. I sniff experimentally, and I'm surprised that it isn't a cold, damp stone I smell. The air has a vegetation odour, which I associate with the earth dweller, but it has a hint of organic decay to it, too, and I wonder if it's because he's sweating.

I'm impressed by Dwalin's speed. I can follow him standing at my full height of five foot three, and there's headroom. Fin, at five foot seven, and even Griffin, at his height, should be able to stand with no problem. The walls are twenty inches wide, though, so Griffin might have to angle his shoulders. There are uneven and sharp spots in the stone, but given the circumstances of this dig, it is impressive work.

The sliding sound alerts me that someone is coming. The noise is growing closer. I turn so that whoever drops in will have a measure of light and not be hit with a wave of claustrophobia. Fin hits the ground and falls backwards, the same as I did. Her eyes fly open, and she arches her shoulder blades, sticking her chest out. "Ouch."

"Come this way, Fin."

She moves close. "Wow."

"Agreed." I turn to watch Dwalin. The top half of his body is working in a rhythmic digging motion. I touch the side wall as close to where he's digging as I can. It's hot, and I pull my hand away. A combination of friction and magic is charging it. The air isn't hot, though. It's stuffy, but there's a coolness coming off the rocks. I can't see the magic he's using to infuse the rock and whatever other magic he's applying to dig into the tunnel he's forming. It doesn't matter anyway because burrowing isn't something a Spellbinder can do. Not only do we not possess the right magic for it, but our bodies aren't built to do it.

"Griffin is coming." Fin laughs, and I can well imagine why she found those three words funny. I don't respond. Within seconds, her voice is rambling away to Griffin. I can't hear what they're talking about, so I focus on Dwalin's back and follow along behind him. Under different circumstances, this could almost be a relaxing experience given there's no overstimulation from electronics, traffic, and other everyday happenings—claustrophobia aside, as well. I focus on the thrum of Dwalin's digging and let my mind empty of thought. *Breathe in. Breathe out.*

Another three minutes pass. "Mayhem's down here now," Fin says. The conversation behind me resumes. I block it out and watch Dwalin and his digging.

It isn't apparent at first, but I soon realize that Dwalin is angling up with his digging, so we are on a modest incline. "Are we getting closer to the crematorium, Dwalin?" I ask.

"Indeed." Stopping, Dwalin turns to face me. "Can you tell them to stop talking now? I've reached the exterior wall of the crematorium, and I need to focus on breaking through it with speed and safety."

I nod and spin toward Fin, who hasn't stopped walking. She bumps into me and grabs on. I roll my eyes and push her back so she's upright again. "Dwalin needs us to stop talking. He's going to break through the crematorium wall now."

There's a deafening crack, followed by a rumbling grunt and a crash. Dust from the broken concrete puffs up into the air. Fin and I both yank the front of our shirts up over our noses and mouths. I spin, coating my body in magic—spark paralyzer orbs in my hands—and move to the opening. The light from inside the room makes the concrete dust look like dancing ash.

Dwalin has gone through the wall without waiting. Jumping through, I dive to the left, not wanting to stay directly in line with the opening we've created. I push against a stainless steel surgical cabinet, using it as a cover in case of an immediate attack from whoever is in the room. It's a sterile room full of metal furnishings, an autopsy table, what I assume is a body cooler, and the cremator. The stink of antiseptic and death is sickening. I push aside unpleasant thoughts and search for Kyson.

The webs of a magic net like the one Kyson used on Cian and Brynlee have ensnared Dwalin. Earth dweller magic isn't the same as Spellbinder magic, though, and his magic isn't completely cut off from him. Regardless, he's struggling. Griffin comes through the wall and charges at a Spellbinder. Based on that Spellbinder's shape, I'm guessing it's Ruck—who was moving an insertion trolley with a casket on it. Fists are flying, and magic is sparking between them.

Scanning, I notice Rye in an open casket. She's awake, wide-eyed. She's tied up with normie zip-ties, a gag in her mouth, and her magic is bound. The weaves binding her are fused with the casket. Her eyes dart to my right to something blocked by the cabinet I'm using for cover. Mayhem startles me by crowding in beside me. I put my hand up in a wait motion and I pop my head out and in from our hiding spot.

"Belamey and Brynlee are here. They're tied to chairs and cut off from their magic. Brynlee's head has sunk to her chest," I whisper to Mayhem. The image of Brynlee's severed finger and fingernails flashes in my mind. *Unconscious. Please let her be unconscious.* There's a table full of knives and tortuous-looking items positioned close to Belamey. Kyson is standing over the table, sneering at the other unexpected visitors in his crematorium. He hasn't seen me. He's watching the opening in the wall. I note Fin has stayed in the tunnel. *Stay there, Fin. Please stay there for a few more minutes.*

Mayhem is watching me, waiting for my lead. I signal her to wait again, then launch air orbs at Belamey and Brynlee, which knocks their chairs over. There isn't time for me to pay attention to whether either of them hits their heads or gets hurt. Instead, I immediately launch another orb, a death orb this time, at Kyson.

I watch the copper-coloured electricity pulsate through the greenish grey orb as it spins toward him. Feeling its energy vibrating like a static cling as it pulls farther from me, I realize that if it connects with Kyson, my death orb will extract a toll on me I wasn't aware of—perhaps most Spellbinders aren't. A distressing feeling—impulsiveness, aggression, paranoia, insanity—is building with each pulse of the orb, but there's a pleasurable sensation, a dopamine release, that works to reinforce the behaviour.

Terror and anger flow through me. *If I can't sever the connection to the orb, it might kill me, too. If it doesn't kill me, it will put me on a path toward dark magic and an evil version of me.* My chest loosens and my breathing eases. *If killing Kyson means I must die, too, then so be it. My friends and family will finally be safe. And if I don't die, then my friends will know how to help me.*

I suck a cleansing breath and smile at Kyson. His expression makes my smile grow bigger. "I got you."

Chapter 21

When I hit Belamey and Brynlee with air orbs, it was a tip-off to Kyson that an attack was coming because he dodged my orb. The result is that the death orb hits the wall instead of Kyson. It fizzles out, having no living matter to act on. The pull it had on me vanishes with no lasting effect. The scorched starburst mark it leaves on the wall is smoking, and the sharp stench reminiscent of an electrical fire lingers—the stink of the orb and not real electrical combustion. My resolve is firm, though; Kyson must die.

Something in my brain reminds me that Belamey, Brynlee, and Ryc are still easy targets. I fling release orbs at the spot where Belamey and Brynlee's chairs tipped over. Since I don't have a direct line of sight on them, and I can't see the weaves that bind them, it's a shot in the dark that I get it correct. But I have no time to worry about it. Kyson lobs a death orb of his own at me.

His failed attempt at hitting me—a gross miss—tells me I startled him with my choice of orb. His forehead wrinkles, his eyes straying to the door across the room and then back to me. A decision forms in his mind, and he launches a net designed to capture me and put a temporary block on my magic—the same type of net he used on Cian and Brynlee. Even though the net's compact nature and the way it unravels like it's a living entity surprise me, I counter with a netted weave that has a vaporizing element included. The speed with which I respond surprises me as much as it surprises him. When our two magics collide, there's a hiss, and both nets disappear. The two magics cancelled each other out.

When I see movement coming from Belamey's tipped chair, I realize that I was successful in freeing him. *Thank goodness.* There is no movement from Brynlee . . . yet. Griffin's yelling during his battle with Ruck, like using his voice will make the impact of his magical strikes more powerful and intimidating. I know there's no way Griffin can overtake Ruck alone, although I'm curious as to how Nyoka's control of him works when she's been captured and is in a state of suspended animation. Unless Ruck picked a side . . . but . . . the cuffs and buckle restrict her ability to use magic. *Ruck chose a side. He's working with Kyson!*

I can't abandon my fight with Kyson, though. That would be equally deadly. I don't envy the position Belamey is in. Does he help Rye escape the casket—

she's vulnerable to attack when she's physically and magically bound, defenceless—and let Griffin or me be overcome, or does he pick a battle? But which battle will he join?

I almost forgot that Mayhem was huddled down beside the cabinet when she darts out past me. "I'll get Brynlee out of here," she says.

My new desire to kill Kyson is on me like blood lust; a death orb thrums in my palm. I don't doubt that the orb is fuelling my existing negative attitude toward him. The only thing that would satisfy me more than my orb connecting with him is getting my hands around his neck and choking the life out of him. My hands ache with the desire. I'm alternating now between death orbs and paralytic orbs. Kyson and I remain locked in our battle alone; Belamey has involved himself elsewhere, and I can't spare my attention to look where. My best guess is he's either releasing Rye or helping Griffin fight Ruck.

"It seems I underestimated how similar we are," Kyson sneers. His voice is like glass on my eardrums, but I ignore his effort to get into my head.

His worry is evident in how his gaze continues flicking through the room. Beads of sweat are visible on his forehead, and his eyebrows are drawn together. His muscles are strained. The most telling action is the extra dome he throws up to shield himself. My chest doesn't puff up and I don't feel a hint of smugness. This duel is far from over.

Using his extra layer of protection, Kyson sidesteps to get to the exit. I can't let that happen. I double my efforts. Moving from the cover of the cabinet, and trusting the shields I've added to protect my body, I move toward him. My death orbs are forgotten for the moment. I work to untangle his dome.

He launches a death orb at me, and his lips curl in pleasure. It lands on the top of my head, connecting with the multiple layers of my shields. *Guess I'm getting to find out firsthand if there's a way to protect against a death orb.* I feel layers dying away as the orb works to get to me before the lack of contact with living matter kills it. Pain lances through me, a migraine that blasts down the length of my body. Not death, though. My shields protected me enough to keep me alive.

My vision is spotty, and I'm unprotected. I lack the energy to do more than work through Kyson's dome. If he launches another death orb, I'm done for. Perspiration rolls down my head, stinging my eyes. I push at his dome with my magic, using hooks of magic like a crocheter frogging a pattern. "I'm okay dying if that's what it takes to kill you." *Did I say that out loud, or am I thinking it?*

Kyson works so hard to hold his dome that he can't spare a minute to throw another orb at me. He's still side-stepping toward the exit, though. He's slower, but he's still trying.

Fin isn't in sight, but I can hear her yelling. She's entered the room, and she's stomping her feet while she hollers. She isn't in pain. *Is she trying to draw someone's attention to her?* Her words are distant in my aching head, something about her creativity. A string of swear words flows, and I know she's run to the casket

Rye is stuck in. I can't peep in her direction, though; at this point, that's all it would take to lose my grip on my fight with Kyson. He doesn't look in their direction, either.

He locks his dull eyes on me. The flush of his effort emphasizes the scars covering his face and bald head. The power of this short, wiry man is amazing, but there's a sadness to him that manages to tug at me.

Fin's voice bellows, "Influencers!" It's so loud and such a strange thing to yell that both Kyson and I flick our eyes in her direction at the same instant.

In her hands, there's a small square canvas that she must have concealed in her back pants pocket. As I watch, it expands from a five-by-five-inch canvas to one equal in size to the original abstract Influencers painting she created. It keeps growing. *This must be what Grama Pearle gave Fin, a magically enhanced canvas. But why?*

The image painted on it is Fin's new design for the Influencer symbol, which explains the mysterious project she's been working on in her bedroom.

It's still an abstract work of art, but there's no doubt about what it represents this time. She's blended Spellbinders and various birds—bright colours—like they're in different stages of shifting. They form a circle around a dark centre, and within that bleak middle is a pair of elastic handcuffs. The canvas has become so large that all I can see are the tips of Fin's fingers where they curl over the edge of the frame. The Influencer symbol is pulling apart, and The Society of the Blood Wind symbol is faint but visible beneath it, melting.

What kind of magic did Grama Pearle associate with this painting?

Kyson is grunting. When I look toward him, fearing that I've made a fatal mistake, he's flailing his arms, struggling against an invisible suction. He's almost bent in half, trying to claw his way to the door, but the suction from Fin's direction is too strong. *A weaponized painting?*

Without warning, his legs yank out from underneath him, but he stays suspended in the air, flying backwards, feet first. Arms still swinging wildly, he's drawn into the magical canvas.

I'm staring at the canvas, unable to process what is going on, when a second body flies past me and into the painting. *Ruck?* The canvas or something close to it explodes, and the white light from it blinds me. The shockwaves of compressed air from the blast hit me. It's scented like damp stone, and I sense that I'm falling, but I'm too tired to brace for the impact. My brain shuts out all forms of perception: no pain, no sound, no sight, no feeling of any kind.

Chapter 22

The first thing I notice when I wake is that I'm not alone or on a hard floor. I don't sense danger. I'm lying on my right side—clothed, in a bed—and there's a body nestled into the contours of my backside, an arm draped over my waist. Given that Belamey's scent is a pocket of yumminess surrounding me, I know it's him who's with me. I don't jump away like I might have in the past. Instead, I stay in my comfy spot. I feel safe enough to close my eyes and go over what I remember last.

I recall the battle and an explosion. My memory feels foggy. Fin was there. She was yelling craziness and holding her canvas painting of The Influencers' symbol—not the original one from a few days ago, though, but a new one.

The painting!

The canvas pulled Kyson and Ruck in. There was a blinding discharge of light, and I lost consciousness.

I can't remember how I got home to my bed, which makes sense because I wasn't awake. I do an internal scan of my body. Given everything I just went through, I feel whole and as healthy as can be expected. I'm tired, which is understandable. *What about everyone else?*

My body has been tensing and relaxing as I've been working through things. The subtle motions are enough to stir Belamey. His arm tightens, pulling me closer. The result, for me, is light-headedness combined with breathlessness. I hear the deep inhale he takes of my hair. "You're in one piece, Firecracker. We're all in one piece."

My words rush out. "You're okay? Are you hurt? Did Kyson torture you?" I want to roll over and inspect him, but he's holding me tight.

"I'm fine, Firecracker," he says, but his voice wavers.

"Belamey?"

"Kyson tied me up and made a lot of threats, but he never got a chance to act on them." Belamey releases me and stretches, groaning.

I flop onto my back and let out a sigh of relief. The weight on the bed fluctuates as Belamey rolls over on top of me. My eyes fly open, and I blink up at him. He pauses with a smirk. "I'm just trying to get off the bed, Firecracker." He winks. "I think you keep it pushed against this wall so you can get me on top of y—"

The door creaks open, and Fin's head pops in. "OHH! That's promising."

"Not anymore," Belamey says with disappointment

as he climbs off me and the bed. He tugs the pillow from under my head and whips it toward her. She ducks out the door and then pops in with the pillow, trying to act abashed.

"Sorry, I can turn soft music on to reset the mood if you like." She inspects Belamey and me.

Belamey stretches and yawns. "Is there coffee?"

Fin smiles big and nods. Belamey scoots out of the room, and Fin dances her shoulders at me. I grab the other pillow and throw it at her. She hops out of the way, laughing. "Come on, Kori. Let's get coffee. We have an apartment full of people."

"Should we cook breakfast?" I ask, swinging my feet over the side of the bed.

"Nope."

"What? Why?"

"Mayhem is cooking. She says she's thinking about pursuing culinary training."

I raise my eyebrows and stand. "Okay, anything that I need to know before I go into the kitchen? Like, how did I get here?"

Fin waves her hand at me. "Nah. We all got knocked out by the explosion of the canvas closing off. Maybe explosion isn't the right word, perhaps blast or discharge. Anyway, my best guess is the canvas pushed outward to keep any of the rest of us from being sucked in as it was closing. You know, Grama Pearle, she has an overzealous flare to her." She grins at her assessment of Grama Pearle. "After the explosion, or whatever it was, we came to one at a time. You took the longest, we assume, because of your proximity to the canvas." She turns to leave.

"Fin?" Spinning, she regards me with her head tipped to the side but says nothing. "What was the canvas stuff?"

"Portal magic," she says and walks away. *Portal magic? Like the shimmering manholes that provide* short-range conveyance? I recall the shimmering manholes we used during the Ember stone battle, but the canvas didn't have that same shimmering stardust look.

I sigh and focus skyward. As I'm about to leave my room, I discover that someone—Fin—has replaced the picture I hang over my bed with Fin's first attempt at painting The Influencer symbol. No point in asking her why it's hanging in my room; she'll have some smartass comment about sexual inspiration. I pause, assessing it. *How did you discern a finger and eyes, Fin? There's no question of the sexual nature of this image.* I make a mental note to find where my coffee picture went. I enjoy the pop art Andy Warhol feel it has. Plus, I love coffee.

The kitchen is warm and filled with the odour of baking, bacon, and cheese. "What is that delicious aroma?"

Fin is bouncing on her toes. "Mayhem's cheddar and bacon biscuits."

"It smells heavenly, Mayhem. Thank you." I wince at my use of the word heavenly and sigh. My desire for further attempts at conversation is non-existent.

She smiles but dips her eyes. I know we're all feeling the ghost of Dodo in the kitchen without any of us having to say the words. Moving to the coffeemaker, I pour myself a generous mug of the dark brew. I can see into the living room where Belamey and Griffin are drinking coffee on the sofa with Dwalin.

Rye is sitting at the breakfast bar with Brynlee beside her. I give Rye a fast eye but know that she would use her ability to alter her appearance to hide any injury or tiredness she's suffering from. Brynlee doesn't have the same skill. Her hands, resting on the counter, clutch a mug of coffee. The bandage on her right hand covers the spot where her pointer finger should've been. My stomach churns. Brynlee's right hand has fingernails on the remaining fingers, but her left hand is missing two fingernails. *Kyson sent us one. He must have been preparing to send us another one.* She has no other visible injuries.

Her eyes have dark circles, and she's lost inside her mind. If she knows I'm in the kitchen, she hasn't acknowledged it. I set my coffee down, walk past Rye—giving her a shoulder squeeze—and wrap my arms around Brynlee.

Her hands move from the warmth of her mug with hesitation, and she bends her arms at the elbows and holds my arms. We just stay that way. "I'm not ready to talk about it," she says.

I kiss the top of her head and eventually release her. She moves her hands back to her coffee in silence. I get that need to process what doesn't seem real or possible. But she's in the room with us and not isolated, so I feel she just needs some time.

"Rye, I . . . Are you . . ." I sigh. "What happened to

you?"

Her eyes search my face and she nods. "I showed up as you, and only Ruck was waiting. Our exchange of words wasn't pretty, but the details aren't important now. He was acting of his own free will. So, I thought maybe I could reach him, get him to help me, to help us." Rye stares over my left shoulder, her eyes flickering as she remembers. "I pushed too far, bringing up Wimpy and the Fog's deaths, and he snapped."

She shakes her head. "Ruck is strong, physically and magically, but I was holding my own. The problem was I was so focused on him that by the time I realized Kyson had arrived, it was too late. He netted me, which forced the shift, revealing my indigo bunting and not your hummingbird. His anger was . . . he was jabbing my body with a knife, small cuts that hurt but weren't deadly. But he started jabbing faster and deeper, like a frenzy. I thought he was going to kill me right there." She stops talking, staring again over my shoulder.

"But he didn't. Why?" I ask softly.

She looks directly at me. "He used healing magic to stop my bleeding because he decided . . ." She swallows, and her words falter. "He decided to cremate me . . . alive." Her eyes fill with tears as she twists her wedding band. I understand she's thinking of Cian.

Cian and Dodo. Bile rises in the back of my throat, and I clench my jaw. I place my hands over Rye's, trying to infuse comfort. "We don't know . . ." I whisper, unable to finish, but the words "how they died" hang in the air unspoken. Rye places her other hand over mine, a gesture of comfort, but says nothing else. She slides her hands away and reaches for her coffee.

I feel like I've ripped open a wound that's never going to heal. I don't know what to say or do. The energy in the apartment is one of overall tiredness and grief. Fin is chatting away at Mayhem, trying to entice her into a conversation, when I pick my coffee up and move to the living room. I plop down on the sofa beside Belamey, and he slips an arm around me. Resting my head against his shoulder, I close my eyes and clutch my coffee.

I'm not focused on what they're talking about. I sip my coffee, just letting their words act as white noise while my thoughts race. *Cian is gone. What does that mean for us, The Influencers? Who leads us? Do we need a leader? Do we need The Influencers?*

The weight of my coffee cup slides from my hands. I don't open my eyes to see who took it. I assume it was Belamey. I don't move; I just let sleep overcome me.

Groggy, the sound of a voice penetrates my mental fog. My neck feels cramped from sleeping on a tilt. I'm not sure what length of time I've been napping for, but I'm aware of the rhythmic rise and fall of Belamey's chest because I'm still leaning against him. Listening to the voices, not so much their conversation but the white noise of it, and I note there's a voice that wasn't here earlier—Grama Pearle!

I slide off the sofa, trying not to disturb Belamey's slumber, noting that Griffin is passed out on the sofa's other end. As I scurry to the kitchen, I can't help smiling. "Kori," Grama Pearle says, opening her arms wide. I race into them and hug her. The strength of her thin arms is welcome but not surprising.

"When? How?" I sputter, stepping away from her to survey her state. She looks tired and dirty, but otherwise she appears the same as always.

She laughs, "I arrived not too long ago. I've been here for two hours, maybe." Her eyes flick to the living room.

"Don't," I say. "You're as bad as Fin."

"Hey, I enjoy being bad," Fin cuts in. "Besides, you shouldn't use that as a measuring stick for Grama Pearle since she's where I learn most of my mischief from."

I glare at the pair of them, a duo of trouble, and shake my head. "How—"

"Travelled by the earth dweller system," Grama Pearle peers at Rye. "That's a fun experience, eh?"

I can't tell if she's being typical Grama Pearle honest or sarcastic. But it doesn't matter. That wasn't what I was going to ask. "I meant . . . how did you get out of the Allurist Detention Centre so quickly? I thought . . ."

"Well, the earth dwellers and I had a chat and made some changes. We came to the surface to get those things started as soon as Kyson and Ruck were delivered to us through Fin's magic painting." Grama Pearle raises her eyebrows and points at Fin. "I outdid myself with the magic I infused that painting with," she says. "Kori, to update you, I'm going to give you answers based on the questions you missed Fin asking.

"The painting would need to be infused with magic again if we were to need another portal. Yes, the magic is similar to manholes, but with two differences. I added a suction to pull negative energy, which was a bit of a gamble, but it worked, so we won't dwell on the ways it could have gone wrong. And I had the magic tied to me so that what or whoever got pulled through would come to me when the portal opened. I suspected I would be at the Allurist Detention Centre. As soon as I heard Nyoka escaped, I figured I would be going there at some point, so I prepared the canvas as a precaution. Oh, and yes, the discharge at the end was something I added too, like a fail-safe to make sure nobody was trying to move through the portal when it closed."

My mouth drops open. "Wait," my head is spinning around the room. Dwalin is nowhere to be seen, and if Grama Pearle travelled underground, then there should be another earth dweller here.

"Gone," Rye says, catching on that I'm searching the room for Dwalin and Grama Pearle's earth dweller guide. "The earth dwellers took Nyoka back with them to the Allurist Detention Centre. Before you ask, Brynlee went home. She wanted to ask if her mother could heal her quicker. She made a half-hearted joke about trying to regrow her finger. Anyway, she said she'll return later."

Two other names pop into my mind, and I struggle with which person I should inquire about first, Blake or Mayhem. "What happens with Blake? He wasn't in the crematorium, and he wasn't innocent in everything that happened, so . . ." I let the question of his consequences hang unspoken before I rush into my next question. "And where is Mayhem?"

Fin gives a strangles groan. "I forgot about Blake. We can't have a mini Kyson wannabe running free. Wait, do we think he's a wannabe?"

Grama Pearle and Rye are both shaking their heads no. Grama Pearle purses her lips as Rye answers. "Blake is young and impressionable, so if we can find him, he will answer for his crimes, but Pearle and I think with the right treatment and attention, there's hope for him."

"Find him?" I ask.

"Yeah, we think he's scared and hiding. We're looking. He'll turn up," Rye says.

I nod. "And where's Mayhem?"

Fin's eyebrows wiggle. "She's down at Just Flavours, trying out the kitchen. We're supposed to go down in a bit for a late lunch. And Grama Pearle spoke to your mom. We're going to your folk's house for dinner. They want to hear about everything face-to-face."

Rye's voice is gentle when she says, "We've planned to have a joint celebration of life for . . ." her voice cracks, "Cian, Dodo, and Ague at the end of the week." Her tone changes, and she swings the bar stool to face me. "Kori."

"Yes?" I can't help the strain in my voice; I feel a bit unsettled by the change in Rye's tone. "What is it?"

"Kori, Cian was planning to step down and pass his position as The Recruiter on to . . ." she pauses, searching my face, but I've no idea what she's looking for. "You."

I stagger from her words, not sure how to process them. "That must be a mistake, Rye. I . . . he . . ."

"No mistake." She faces the breakfast bar and picks up her cup of coffee. The conversation is over. If there was more to tell, she'd say.

"Holy shit, boss." Fin thumps me on the back. When I gaze at her, she smiles. "Can I have a raise?"

"Fin." I roll my eyes and turn to walk away. I need to process this—alone.

"Kori, I'm getting married. I have a dress to buy, service providers to hire, cake to taste test. Wait, does cake tasting cost money? Kori, I need more funds." She isn't following me, so I don't worry about the need to force the door closed to keep her out. I shut it, muffling Fin's voice, and slide down to the floor, lost and unsure about all of it.

Chapter 23

I stay slumped on the floor for a while. My bones hurt from the strange position, and my brain aches from the processing. "Time to shower," I tell myself. The thought of hot water and a steam-filled room fills my whole body with yearning. I haven't come to a complete acceptance of what I've been told. The responsibility is so great. *The Recruiter? Me?* I clamber off the floor and into the kitchen.

Griffin and Belamey have joined the group at the breakfast bar. They all turn to watch as I enter. I can tell by their silent assessment of me they were discussing Cian's last wishes. Their faces don't register surprise.

"Good timing," Fin says. I raise my eyebrows but keep moving toward the bathroom as she speaks. "We were just getting ready to go downstairs to eat."

"Okay. I want to grab a shower, and then I'll come meet you guys." Slipping into the bathroom, I close the door and turn the water on. I remove my clothes and drop them on the floor. The steam fogs up the bathroom mirror. I don't feel my usual need to peer into the reflective glass and see if it's still me staring back. I know it is. Nodding to myself, I pull the shower curtain and step in. I'm ready for this challenge.

The stream of water that's beating against my flesh is stinging where it hits, a combination of force and heat. "I'm The Recruiter," I say out loud before I close my eyes and tip my head up.

The rustle of the curtain doesn't startle me, but I silently wish I'd taken the time to install the hook and eye ring so I could lock the door. Fin has her ideas about what makes a conversation an emergency and where conversations should happen, and she has an inability to be patient about having them.

I don't open my eyes or move my head out of the shower spray. "Fin, can I please just have my shower and come down for food after?"

"It's not Fin." Belamey's husky voice is not what I was expecting, and I freeze. I sense he's behind me in the shower. *Naked.* My mouth goes dry. Suddenly, it seems like I can feel each bead of water on my body, and despite the heat, my skin pimples with goosebumps.

My voice is low. "Bclamey?"

"I can leave . . . if you want me to."

I shake my head no, not trusting myself to formulate coherent words. He moves closer to me, and I tremble. The backs of his fingers trail down my arms as he speaks. "Turn?" It's a question, not a command.

The dryness in my mouth has turned moist, and my breath hitches. I turn, unhurried, and lock my eyes on his deep brown ones.

"I knew your feelings would catch up," he says as his lips press softly against mine. It's a teasing kiss, and he pulls his lips away.

I search his face.

He gives me another fleeting kiss. This time, he moves his mouth away just enough to ask me one last question. "Are you ready for us?"

"Yes," I whisper.

I'm The Recruiter. I'm ready for anything.

Please turn the page for a bonus short story—
occurring before The Ember Files—from Shari
Marshall.

A Prick of Magic

An Ember Files Short Story

Chapter 1

The heat of the day clings to the night breeze. Kinsley doesn't mind. Instead, she takes advantage of the thermal currents to preserve the energy in her long, pointed wings. She knows she's a sexy bird, the same way she knows she's a sexy woman; she's going to knock them dead—literally and figuratively. *Kinsley*, she thinks, trying on her new name like a pair of work-issued cargo pants. If she wasn't in bird form, her complexion would be ruddy, her grin wide, and her laughter throaty.

Life is painful. More people need to realize that, and Kinsley decided long ago that she would help others reach that understanding. Destroying—or at least incapacitating—the one family of Spellbinders she hates most will be immensely satisfying. It'll also be rewarding because it puts her one step closer to becoming the Spellbinder with the most control and influence. It's step one of her plans: create a bit of scandal, destroy a few lives, kill a couple of people, and get laid along the way—seems like a successful tour of duty.

Step two isn't clear, but it'll come to her. Since it involves some kind of attack on The Society of the Blood Wind, a society that lives by a system of heinous ideas that places normies as inferior to Spellbinders, Kinsley will need to be prepared. Their society runs on fear and dark secrets.

Dolion Adelgrief, the head of The Society of the Blood Wind, can't find out Kinsley's in the area. His hate for her isn't strong enough to search her out and destroy her, but if he discovers she's close to his home, then it'll be a different story. Kinsley doesn't want to dwell on that right now. She'll figure out how to deal with Dolion, his son Nekane, and The Society of the Blood Wind later. One aspect of the mission at a time, and the Ember family is first.

Excited by her thoughts, Kinsley's flight pattern is erratic. She makes a short, deep "terk" sound, typical of a northern carmine bee-eater, and snatches a flying insect out of the air with her black decurved beak before refocusing her attention.

The lights of the Lindsay, Ontario, community she's destined for glow in the distance. With a population of just over 22,000, this won't be the most exciting posting she's given herself, but it's a small price to pay.

Setting up an assumed identity here didn't require a lot of effort. All it took was some mind control and the manipulation of a few normies. Most normies are easy to manipulate, and the ones Kinsley exploited didn't prove any different. Any species that can convince itself not to see something that's right in front of it has a pliable brain, one that is susceptible to enchantment. Normies live in a world of magic but waste the beauty of it by comprehending it through a lens of science, superstition, coincidence, and fictional stories. They don't believe magic exists.

Kinsley flies straight to the duplex she's renting. The lights, set on timers, have come on, giving the three windows on the narrow house front a soft orange glow. Not wanting to have any nosey normies to deal with, Kinsley rented both the upper and lower units of the house. She'll live on the main floor for the time it'll take to complete her mission. The long-shaped house was recently renovated with grey vinyl plank floors and pale grey walls. Since grey is Kinsley's favourite colour, the house is a perfect choice.

She swoops toward the small porch and shifts, landing her trim, one-hundred-and-thirty-pound body with precision. She taps the lock with her finger, unlocking it with a zap of magic, and strolls into her sparsely furnished home. The sweet, almost honey-like smell of jasmine fills the house from the glass bottle diffusers Kinsley requested the landlord scatter throughout the main floor. She inhales, long and deep, feeling its calming effects and the edge it gives her alertness.

She's set herself up for a long operation. She can't be sure how long it will take her to get pregnant, and that is an important part of this plan. She starts her new job as a fake police officer in the morning, part of the deception she's going to be living. It disappoints Kinsley that the normies in such regarded positions of power aren't harder to bend to her will. It cost her no effort to fabricate her resume and position as an experienced police officer at their detachment. Their minds just accepted it. Regardless, the memory gives her a heady rush of power and an unkind smile slides across her face. "I might as well celebrate that with a drink," she purrs.

She pulls a crystal tumbler from the cabinet by the fridge, the solid glass a satisfying weight in her hand. She grabs the vodka from the freezer, admiring the frostiness of the bottle. Estimating two ounces as she pours, she works mechanically, putting the bottle back in the freezer and adding ice cubes, lemon juice, simple syrup, and grenadine.

Trance-like, she stares at the drink's red hue. Unwittingly, the chill of the glass triggers thoughts of her parents and the death chills that set into their bodies in the hours following their demise. Kinsley's Spellbinder parents—although she wasn't Kinsley then—were always too happy and too perfect. Their flawlessness felt unnatural and impossible for a child, and then a young girl, to live up to.

In private, her parents were never good at hiding their disgust with her. Her father would curl his lip and look away from Kinsley and her mistakes. When she would ask him about it, his answers were evasive. But her mother's responses hurt the most; a constant recoiling from Kinsley's imperfections—small things like ice cream dripping on her clothes—coupled with a pained expression. Her mother's eyes shifted between judgment and frigidity.

Kinsley didn't witness their murder, but when she found them lifeless with their eyes open—cold, dead eyes—she wasn't uncomfortable. That was how they often looked at her, with dispassion and scorn.

Kinsley sat with their bodies for hours, noting that the persistent feelings of shame and self-doubt she normally felt in their presence weren't there. She wasn't nauseous. Her mouth wasn't dry, and her heart wasn't racing. She sat popping sour cherries into her mouth, and for the first time in her life, she didn't feel like an imposter.

It was after their deaths that she decided to become someone new, someone of her choosing. So, she started living under the surname Reun. She thought her spelling was clever; it was one of the first decisions she made after her parent's death and she has an emotional attachment to the name that she can't explain—maybe it's as simple as taking charge of her life so she never again feels like her parents made her feel. That connection keeps her from changing the spelling to avoid the irritation she feels every time somebody pronounces it incorrectly. For her first name, she alternates between alias. Kinsley is a new name, and it might be one she uses again if the mood strikes her.

Kinsley shrugs, breaking her trance. She pulls the fridge open and pulls out a small dish of Montmorency sour cherries she paid the landlord to stock in her fridge a few days ago. The bright red of the cherries' skin makes her smile. She holds a round, medium-sized cherry to her mouth and sinks her front teeth into it. Her cheeks pucker in response to the sourness. She inspects the yellow flesh inside before putting the rest of the cherry into her mouth, manoeuvring it so her teeth and tongue can detach the pit, which she spits into the bowl. "Fresh Ontario cherries are one good thing about this operation," she muses.

She eats a couple more cherries and places the bowl back in the fridge. Scooping her drink off the counter makes the ice cubes tink against the glass. The cold liquid flows over her tastebuds, tart and refreshing. She downs the contents, puts the glass in the dishwasher, and heads off to bed. She's falling asleep feeling eager about acting as a cop: Constable Kinsley Reun. *Nobody will pronounce Reun as re-oon,* her sleep brain says. *Reun will be pronounced ruin as in destruction. It has always been a fitting surname for me.*

Chapter 2

The mingled odours of freshly brewed coffee, chai, and cider cling to the air inside Just Flavours. It's Kinsley's third shift as a police officer, and she's standing at the till, waiting for her coffee order. The whir of the coffee bean grinder, clinking spoons, background music, and muted conversation create a backdrop of noise. Kinsley is reading the chalkboard specials, her back to the café's entrance. She doesn't notice Kori Ember and Fin Salinger enter the café, but Fin notices Kinsley.

Fin throws a soft elbow into Kori's side. "Look at that cop. Her uniform highlights her curves. She must be the new cop at the neighbouring police service." Fin tips her head sideways. "Except for her Kool-Aid-coloured hair, this one is hot to trot."

Kori rolls her eyes. "How did you hear there was a

new cop?"

"I was on a date last night with a policeman." Fin dances her eyebrows. "Who it was doesn't matter. It only matters that he didn't pass the audition. And yes, I'm talking about a sexual audition. Anyway, he mentioned a new cop, Kinsley R-something, and she has a name fixation. Whatever that means." Fin's eyes twinkle. "Let's meet her."

"What? Why?"

Fin turns toward Kori and mimes pulling a pair of glasses down her nose. With her chin tipped to her chest, Fin looks over those imaginary glasses at Kori. Fin leaves her fingers by the side of her eye like she's pinching the arm of her pretend frames. She does it so well that Kori can almost visualize the glasses. Kori snorts.

Fin steps in close to Kori and lowers her voice. "Listen, Kori, Kool-Aid cop is a new female in town. Eligible bachelors are already limited, and not all of us are married to our dream man like you are."

"So?" Kori asks, shifting her eyes to the Kool-Aid cop.

Fin grimaces and her voice comes out strained. "I'll break it down for you. This cop chick is either friend-worthy—and by that, I mean she's either married, a lesbian, celibate, or some combination of those categories—or she's a rival."

"You do know that you're offensive sometimes, Fin?"

Fin shrugs. "Let's meet her."

Kinsley turns, a pinched expression on her face, as she tries to leave with her coffee. Fin steps in Kinsley's way and gives her a big smile.

Kinsley narrows her eyes and clenches her jaw, apparently upset that we might interrupt her coffee break with a police-related problem. "Can I help you?" Her posture is rigid.

"You're the new officer from the police station on the other side of Angeline Street, right?" Fin leans toward the Kool-Aid cop's breast to read the Velcro name tag. "Constable Re-oon?"

Kinsley's lips pull into a forced smile, and her tone is sharp. "It's pronounced 'Ruin.' Think of devastation, demolish, or destroy. Ruin." Her eyes swing toward Kori and away, but she does a double-take before focusing on Fin. "What did you need, ma'am? I've got a call to attend."

"My name is Fin, Constable Ruin." Fin carefully pronounces the letters. "I just wanted to say hi. You know, be friendly to the new girl in town—"

"Re-oon," a male voice hollers from the doorway. "Hustle, we have a break-and-enter in progress."

"It's 'RUIN.'" Kinsley brushes past Fin and out the door, following her partner.

Kori watches the door close. "What was that? Did she smile at me or snarl?"

Fin is nodding. "That one's going to be a problem." She gives a bark of laughter. "Ruin. Someone has a goddess complex."

Carter can hear his wife, Kori Legand, although nobody calls her Legand. She's an Ember and always will be, no matter how hard she tries to escape it. It makes her furious. Carter can tell by the tone of her voice that she's angry now, although it'll be for different reasons than her surname. Kori functions at a low smoulder, at least where work—not work politics—is concerned, which has earned her the nickname "Smouldering Ember."

Thinking about the other ways Kori smoulders, Carter enters the bullpen—the main administration area where police officers sit to complete their mountains of paperwork—and he scans for Kori. They work opposite rotations and sometimes get to see each other at the changeover. The familiar smell of stale coffee, gunmetal, and body odours is welcoming to Carter, and he puffs up his five-nine and one-hundred-and-sixty-five-pound self like a peacock. He looks good in civilian clothes, but with the uniform on, he's at a whole different level.

Kori's yelling has stopped. The clicking of fingers moving over keyboards and the drone of conversation create a pleasant white noise. Nobody is paying much attention to a constable and a corporal's customary argument.

Kori's in the doorway to the corporal's office, standing with her shoulders back, chest out, and hands on her hips. The blinds covering the glass window to Corporal Gage Cogburn's office are open, and Carter gets a clear view of Corporal Cogburn's scarlet face. The corporal's eyes pop. His cheeks puff with air, and even from ten feet away, Carter notices the beads of sweat on the corporal's forehead, as well as the neck vein that looks like it's about to explode. He's wildly shaking a pair of black work boots at Kori.

Carter surveys Kori's athletic five-foot-three body. Her short, sassy hair is in a stubby ponytail. She's wearing her bulletproof vest, which is miserable in the summer heat. A duty belt with a gun, radio, and baton is visible. He knows her pepper spray and spare magazines sit on the front of her belt. She's dressed in cargo-issue work pants with a Taser on her left thigh. This part of her uniform isn't what Kori and the corporal are arguing about, but Carter has no illusions about that. He knows without looking at Kori's feet that she's either barefoot or wearing sandals; she's preferred being barefoot for as long as he's known her.

"They're work sandals," Kori bellows with a foot stomp.

Corporal Cogburn closes his eyes. The work boots are at eye level in his outstretched hand, but he's stopped shaking them. Kori turns to leave, and she deftly bobs the top half of her body to the side as one boot goes sailing past where her head was seconds previous. Because footwear is a routine argument between Kori and her corporal, she expects the boot throw.

"Cops don't get issued SANDALS with their kit!" Cogburn thunders, spit spraying from the corners of his mouth. The other boot flies out of his hand and smacks the door frame, dropping to the floor with a thud.

"Burn your suspension and firebomb your silly rules!" Kori says, her voice dripping defiance. She walks away.

"They aren't MY rules!" Corporal Cogburn crosses his office in three angry steps. "And why can't you use the fucking swear words every other cop uses?" He slams his office door and drops the blinds. The closed door only mutes the sounds of him cussing and banging things.

"F . . . f-fiery blazes." Kori's amber eyes are lit with a copper tint and glow with her anger.

When Kori sees Carter, he finger-combs his brown hair and waits for her to come to him. He smirks and winks. "You are the most normal weird person I know." His words are breathy. Carter freezes, and his eyes widen. "Holy shit, I sound like Fin," he mutters with a shaky voice.

Kori laughs at Carter's shocked reaction to making a Fin-like comment. Finley Salinger, also known as Fin, is Kori's best friend. Fin and Carter have a relationship built on mutual over-the-top teasing. Usually, they obey the rules of playfulness, but sometimes they border on hurtful. Kori stays out of their mockery, preferring to watch from the sidelines. She refuses to pick sides between her best friend and her husband.

Carter has yet to recover from Fin mocking him for lacking friends outside the police department. In his mind, Carter can hear Fin's laughing words: "To the gym with Constable Davis Stanway or to the gun range with Constable Jeff Toffton. Sad man, Carter, you're a sad man. Do you refer to each other by first name, or do you keep the cop rank? Get some real friends, dude."

Kori rises onto her toes in front of Carter, and they brush lips, breaking Carter's brooding. She drops back onto her feet and watches him straighten his vest. No words pass between them, and he heads off to start his night shift.

The warmth outside is like a wall when Carter exits to the back parking lot to get into his police vehicle. Something feels off. He doesn't know what it is, but the unease has the hairs on the back of his neck prickling. He stops in the middle of the hot parking lot, the smell of the asphalt drifting toward him as the sounds of a road crew doing repairs up the street reach his ears.

There are no people in his immediate vicinity. The police radio on his left hip is silent, and the sky is blue and cloudless—there's nothing untold to explain why he feels on edge. Carter, still standing in the same spot in the parking lot, reaches into the front pouch of his vest and pulls out a small container of green Tic Tacs, enjoying the gentle clicking of the little pill-shaped candy. Smiling, he pops two in his mouth, appreciating the smooth feel of them on his tongue and the way the sweet, minty flavour calls up pockets of saliva.

Ready to get his shift started, he moves toward his police car again. With his first step, his foot squishes down and sticks enough that he realizes the resistance he feels is someone's spit-out piece of chewed gum. His smile is gone as he stomps the rest of his way to his car. The slight crinkle of his nose is the only recognition he allows as he opens the car door to a fart bomb smell. A stinky police vehicle is a common occurrence, and he wonders what people are eating to create such a lingering nasty odour. He logs into his mobile workstation and reads the first call of his night shift.

There are no lights and sirens required as Carter drives across town for a disturbance call. The dispatch ticket reads that a man is yelling about being a bird. Carter feels confident that he's going to find the man with the crazy-speckled eyes and the short, thick neck. The detachment has been getting calls about this man; he's been causing a public display at least once a month for the last six months. If Carter didn't know better, he would think that the man acts out, hoping Kori will be the responding officer when someone makes a complaint. The man often asks for Constable Ember, not Legand, but Ember.

"Anybody have eyes on the bird man, yet?" Carter asks over the police radio.

After a brief pause, an unfamiliar but pleasant female voice responds. The sound of wind rushing past the radio, coupled with fast footfalls, indicates the unknown female cop is in pursuit on foot. "Male running down Angeline Street past the hospital toward

Colborne. He's short and thick-set. He's wearing jeans and a black T-shirt."

The thing with the bird man is that he typically just needs a stern warning to quiet down and go home. He hasn't run before. So, either it isn't the bird man, or something different is going on with him tonight.

Angeline Street is the border that separates police jurisdictions. Carter works for the police service that deals with in-town crime, while out-of-town crime is the responsibility of another police service. Angeline Street is sometimes a bone of contention regarding who should respond to calls for service, but when it comes to officer safety—any officer—they all back each other up. The two police services rarely share a police radio channel, but this call was clearly dispatched to both police services, and the constable responding must have switched to the in-town repeater. Carter engages his emergency response equipment and speeds up. When he turns onto Angeline Street, there isn't a person in sight.

The radio crackles to life. "Lost him. He ran into the trees on the park's far side, yelling about a bird's life."

The bird man. Carter turns his police vehicle into the local park just up the street from the hospital, shuts the emergency equipment off, and parks. He climbs out of the car, scanning the park for anything out of the ordinary. A cop with hair that is more pink than red is walking toward him, her hips swaying. Her uniform hugs the toned curves of her body. Carter knows he's staring, but he can't seem to help it. It's like his eyes are glued to her. He isn't even sure he's blinking.

The female officer gives him a toothy smile and bats long eyelashes over her blue eyes. She extends her hand, "I'm Constable Reun."

The act of moving to shake hands breaks the strange hold the officer seems to have on Carter. He smiles. "Constable Ruin, eh? New here?" *That likely explains why the bird man ran; he didn't have a familiar face to deal with.*

Kinsley is pleased that Carter grasped the proper pronunciation of her name, but then again, he isn't reading it off a paper. They're still holding hands, but the shaking action has stopped. So, their arms are awkwardly bent between them. Kinsley takes her free hand and sets it on top of her and Carter's clasped ones. She uses a teeny tack to prick the surface of his flesh. She started planting small suggestions in his mind the moment she realized who he was, which is enough distractive magic to prick him without him noticing. The minuscule amount of potion coating the tip of the tack will be enough to get Kinsley's plan rolling.

"Yes, I'm new here. Well, I'm new to the police service on the other side of Angeline Street," Kinsley says. "I patched over from a different police service, but it's my second week on the job here." She lowers her voice to nearly a whisper. "And you are?"

Carter is aware of an increase in his saliva and the quickening of his breath. *She's so sexy.* A high-pitched "kik-kik-kik" startles Carter; the frantic sound of the hawk's call resonates through him. He eyes the forest but doesn't see any birds. He yanks his hand back, unaware of the breach to his skin or the magic making its way through his normie body.

"I'm Constable Legand, married," he says without knowing why. He can't decide if he feels confused or embarrassed by his own behaviour. His brain feeling muddled isn't a normal thing for him. "You can call me Carter."

"Kinsley," she says, her eyes searching the sky for the source of the bird's call. Carter notes that her smile, which seconds ago captivated him, has a menacing quality to it.

"Well, it was a pleasure to meet you, Kinsley, but we should probably get back to our sides of the street. The boss frowns on us lingering in the middle for calls or coffee." He turns to leave. She says nothing as she continues looking at the sky. He speaks over his shoulder, "The bird man didn't actually turn into a bird, newbie."

Carter gets into his car. The last hours of daylight are slipping into dusk. He leaves for another service call. He doesn't see Kinsley again that night, but thoughts of her creep involuntarily into his mind. Unbeknownst to Carter, this is the effect of the magic that Kinsley introduced to his system. Over the next seventy-two hours, the magic will embed in his brain, making Kinsley a fixed idea in his mind. The thoughts will be so pervasive that he will shake his head a few times, trying to clear them out.

At the end of his shift, Carter is sitting in the bullpen, staring at his computer monitor. He isn't seeing the words of his report; he's visualizing Kinsley, the pale skin of her hands slowly unbuttoning her uniform shirt.

Davis slams his hand down on Carter's shoulder. "Carter. Shithead, I'm talking to you. I said, are you and your wife coming out for drinks this weekend?"

"My wife?"

"Fuck man, did someone blow cocaine in your face? Yes, your wife. Are you and Kori coming out for drinks tonight?"

Carter looks at the white-gold wedding band on his left hand. His stomach clenches, and he gasps, immediately trying to cover it with a fake cough. *What is going on with me?* "Drinks? Probably, I'll check with Kori."

Standing abruptly, he pushes past Davis and heads for the locker room, eager to change and go home. His right hand is spinning his wedding ring around on his ring finger the whole time. *I need to get some sleep.*

Kinsley knows she shouldn't play with her prey, but she needs to have a bit of fun. It's just who she is. She could seduce Carter without magic, but that would take longer. Although she likes to play, she doesn't aspire to be stuck in this community for an extended period. She has to start the scandal, which will weaken the Ember family's public image.

Then there is the question of the bird man. Kinsley is sure he charged into the trees and shifted, which would make him a Spellbinder. But who is he, and what is going on with him? She sneers at the thought of it and pushes it aside as inconsequential—Carter is the focus.

Kinsley didn't plan to meet Carter today at work. She was prepared for the possibility, but her aim had been a bar or coffee shop where she could linger and flirt after drugging him. She made today work, though. On top of administering the potion, Kinsley planted small magic suggestions in his mind so he would think of her. She doesn't understand why the Spellbinder community frowns on mind control and manipulation magic, at least where normies are concerned. What harm can it do to have a little fun with them?

Kinsley wants Carter to reach a state where he seeks her out, and she wants this to happen on her timeline. The combination of the potion and her suggestions will have him hunting for her like a male dog searching for a bitch in heat.

Once Carter comes to her, she'll flirt a bit and push him past the limit. Images of herself pushing up against Carter's toned body, the gentle stroke of their tongues, clothes being removed, limbs entwining . . . Kinsley shivers and the nerve endings in her lady bits tingle and ache. Scowling with impatience, she cuts her shift short. She needs to go find herself a willing sexual play toy to relieve her building carnal aggression.

Chapter 3

Carter enters his home, actively trying not to spin his wedding band. The obsessive desire to touch his ring is new—ever since he met Constable Reun. It's like his subconscious is suffering from guilt about his attraction to her. He isn't expecting Kori to be awake this early. When she says hello, he jumps and stifles a yelp. She doesn't seem to notice as she slides her arms around his waist and presses her body against his. She tips her head up for a kiss.

Kori is soft and warm against his body. Her fingers move playfully along the small of his back. Carter tilts his head down and pushes his lips to hers. He feels the tension drain out of his body. The fog in his brain clears, and he sighs. He can't remember why he was feeling tense.

"I love you," he breathes without pulling out of their

embrace or their kiss. He doesn't jump when the door opens behind him. Kori's mouth stretches into a smile against his lips.

"Gag me," Fin says by way of greeting. "Kori, are you ready to go? Carter, don't turn around because if your prick is standing, I've no desire to see it."

Despite their lips being attached, Carter and Kori smile with their eyes open. They're not surprised by Fin's foul mouth. Kori can see in Carter's eyes that he's considering responses. Kori kisses him again and pulls back, placing her finger against his mouth. "Fin and I are going out of town for a couple of days. I might as well make use of my latest suspension."

"Plus, she can wear sandals or go barefoot for all I care," Fin chimes in.

Carter bends to kiss Kori again. "Have fun. I'll miss you." He straightens and turns to Fin with his arms open.

Fin looks down at the front of Carter's pants. "No woody," she says with a smile. She steps in for a hug. "Either you aren't doing it right, Kori," Fin teases, "or there's something wrong with your penis, you prick."

Kori rolls her eyes at Fin.

"Goodnight, Fin." Carter's voice is indifferent, but when he addresses Kori, there's affection in his tone. "Love you, wife." Carter walks off to the bedroom and showers in a daze. The Air Supply song "Every Woman in the World" runs through his mind as he thinks about Kori—the love of his life, although it would be out of character for him to admit that out loud. The very thought of her brings him contentment.

He's asleep as soon as his head hits the pillow. Sleep steals away his thoughts of Kori. Instead, Carter dreams of a form that's shadowlike and lacks detail. It moves toward him, seductive and evil. He's rooted to the spot, unable to do more than watch and breathe. As the figure closes in, the hairs on his neck prickle with fear.

The shadow changes before his eyes, developing curves and feminine features. The form is so close their noses are touching. Blue eyes with long lashes blink at him. He feels two hands on his chest, warm and slow. They slide down the front of his body, stopping to release the button of his pants. What Carter had felt and defined as prickles of fear moments ago are now tingles of anticipation. He wakes sweating, uncomfortable, and dissatisfied.

Grouchy, Carter moves through the next twelve hours of his shift on autopilot. Knowing he isn't ready to sleep when his shift ends, he stops to get breakfast. He avoids Just Flavours because he doesn't want to run into anyone he'll have to socialize with. He picks a breakfast place on a side street that doesn't draw much traffic. Sliding into a dimly lit booth, he waits for his order while sipping coffee.

Carter leans back in the booth and closes his eyes. A soft, warm hand caresses his cheek. In response, his pulse quickens and his eyes fly open, expecting to see Kori back early from her trip with Fin. But it's Kinsley standing beside his table.

Her pinkish hair is falling around her shoulders. She bats her eyes at him and gives him that snarly smile.

"Hello, Mr. Married," she teases. "Can I join you?"

His eyes scan her body, noting the black tights that hug her curves and the low-cut grey T-shirt that reveals her ample breasts. Kinsley picked this outfit for a reason. Since she isn't actively using magic, she wants to leave as little to Carter's imagination as possible.

His mouth goes dry. *She's so captivating.*

Kinsley doesn't wait for a verbal response. She surprises Carter by sliding into the booth beside him. He pushes over toward the wall to give her space, but Kinsley scootches closer to him so her leg presses against his.

"Rough night? You look tense," she purrs. "I can help you release that tension." Her hand is on his knee, and she drags it up his thigh, pausing before reaching his crotch. Again, she refrains from using any magic or crossing any lines that normie laws would define as sexual assault.

Carter's insides are vibrating. "Tired." His voice cracks with the word. He considers shoving her over on the bench to make space between them but dismisses the notion. *What's a bit of harmless flirting? It's been a long time since a beautiful woman, besides his wife, flirted with him.* His thoughts are fleeting and feel foreign like they aren't his own. "You?"

Kinsley leans in. She deliberately pushes her breasts against Carter's arm. Her cherry, sugar-candy, and jasmine fragrance fills his nose. Carter is having a difficult time focusing. He hooks the collar of his shirt with his finger and runs it back and forth like the shirt has become tight around his neck. Kinsley's voice is low. "My night was lonely."

The server plunks Carter's plate on the table, causing him to jump. Kinsley doesn't move or acknowledge the interruption. "You need anything else, Mister?" the server asks, tapping the long, manicured fingernail of her pointer finger on the table.

Carter doesn't trust himself to speak, so he shakes his head no and watches the server stroll back to the kitchen. His eyes remain locked on the spot where the server was as Kinsley's hot breath tickles his ear with her next words. "I'll be over later tonight." She nips his ear, giving it a gentle tug.

She pulls back just enough to see Carter's face. His mouth is slightly parted from shock and desire. He wiggles on the bench, tugging his pants away from the growing pressure in his groin. Before he can respond, Kinsley's lips are on his. Her tongue pushes between the gap in his mouth, and he groans. He knows something isn't right, but thanks to the magic, he can't organize his thoughts to make sense of what it is.

Kinsley strokes Carter's face with the back of her hand. She can see that she's befuddled him. He's playing into her sexual advances. "Get some sleep, stud. I'll see you at your place in a few hours."

She slides from the booth and turns back to Carter. His head is bobbing yes. She smiles and sighs. "And don't worry about that bitch you call wife." Kinsley walks away, posture perfect and hips swaying. She's pleased with the magical emphasis that she put on the word "bitch." The magic lace will continue to weave into Carter's thoughts and brain patterns to keep him thinking about Kinsley and confused about his relationship with Kori.

If Kinsley were a different person, she might almost feel sorry for the poor dupe. But Kinsley, in the throes of an adrenalin rush, feels only disdain. She takes a few steps outside, shifts, and flies toward her temporary home.

Carter eats his breakfast mechanically. If anybody had been around to pay attention to him, they would have thought he was auditioning for a zombie movie. The only thing he's aware of is his deep exhaustion, which is more exaggerated than normal after a night shift. He wonders if he's getting sick, but that wouldn't explain why he has no memory of paying for his meal or of his commute home. He falls onto the bed and is asleep where he lands.

His sleep is filled with strange dreams about his body being out of his control, moving and acting in ways that both please and shame him. He's naked as the dark and seductive shape from his dream circles him. *Succubus.* He's enveloped in a warm, sweet, fruity, and floral smell. The shadow, human in form, has one detail. Lustrous, wavey pink hair. Carter's waking memory is of himself and the demon copulating.

Carter is restless in the hours that lead up to Kinsley's arrival. *Kori hangs out with male friends. I've hung out with other women before. It means nothing.* He contemplates calling Kinsley to cancel but realizes he has no contact number for her. Calling work to get her number opens the possibility for questions now and later, depending on who he speaks to. He considers not answering the door, but being ill-mannered appalls him. He could leave so he isn't here when she arrives, but that seems rude too.

"She's not a demon, and I'm not planning on having sex with—" The doorbell cuts off Carter's speech to himself. He twists his wedding band as he walks to the door. His chest feels tight as he places his hand on the doorknob. The dark shape with Kinsley's hair from his dream pops into his head. "There isn't a demon on the front porch," he tells himself as he cranks the door open.

He's relieved to see Kinsley has facial features and all the defining details that make her a person. The sight of her pronounced cleavage nestled in the V-neck of her tight graphite-coloured shirt makes his pulse quicken. He stands back to allow her entry, all thoughts of turning her away gone from his mind. She hands him a pizza box and lifts a small bag into his line of sight. She pulls out a bottle of red wine.

"I brought two. I hope you have an opener," she purrs, twisting a lock of hair around a finger.

They fill the next chunk of time with pizza, wine, conversation, and laughter. Kinsley has been the only person occupying his thoughts all night. They've been sitting on either end of the sofa, but they're facing each other. She studies him as much as he studies her. Any unease Carter felt about having Kinsley in the house has passed. Carter knows that he's free with his words and feels flushed. He wouldn't call himself intoxicated, but he also wouldn't operate a vehicle.

"I should probably get going," Kinsley says, standing.

Carter looks up at her. "Already?"

Her lips pull back, showing her teeth. "Well," she says with her head to the side, "there's one thing we haven't done yet."

Carter's mouth has gone dry; his pulse increases. "Oh?"

Kinsley closes the small distance between them and lowers herself onto Carter's lap. Her eyes lock on his as she slowly leans toward his lips. His hands move to her waist, and he aches to caress her. She playfully tugs at his lower lip with her teeth before shifting to trail her tongue up his neck to nibble his earlobe. Her breath is hot on his ear. "Please?"

Everything else falls away as they give their feverish bodies over to one another. No thoughts. Just pleasure.

When Carter wakes the next morning, he leaves his eyes closed, assessing. He has a firm mattress underneath him, a soft pillow cupping his head, and comfy blankets covering him. He doesn't remember making his way to bed. There's a warm body pressed up against his with an arm draped over him. He breathes in. When his brain registers Kinsley's fragrance, his eyes fly open. *What is going on?*

Before he can register more, Kinsley moves up over the top of him, straddling his thighs. She can see the panic in his wide eyes, which start darting around the room, looking for an escape. Her magic isn't wearing off, but extra manipulations implanted in his brain strengthen the magic and help it work fast. His body is radiating tension. If the mattress wasn't underneath him, Carter would back away.

The original magic from the poke to his hand is still in his system, but Kinsley hadn't used extra magic on Carter last night. When she had pricked him during their first meeting in the park, she had embedded thoughts of herself in his mind. She also confused him about his marital status with her mind manipulations, but last night had been about free will and bad—well, good for her—decisions. She can't have Carter's pre-existing beliefs about marriage and social interactions wreck her plan now, and she has no desire to expel any more energy seducing him; she has won that battle already. But she's only started setting the groundwork for the scandal. The chances of her being pregnant after one night of sex are slim. She needs a few more stolen moments. The fact that Carter will remember their time together will help fuel the scandal.

Kinsley leans forward, bracing herself with her

hands on the front of Carter's shoulders. She sends tiny waves of calm magic into him, along with some judgment inhibitors. She's surprised by the ease with which he responds to it. Unfortunately, she feels *all* his muscles relax. She decides she needs to buy time for the magic to balance out in his system. "Let's make some . . ." she trails off, searching for a clock to show the time. The alarm clock on the bedside table says 11:15 a.m. "Let's make brunch. Then I'll share some *dessert* with you before I leave." She takes extra care to infuse the word *dessert* with sexually suggestive magical notes.

Carter is slow to get out of bed. He pulls on loose-fitting studio pants before he exits the room. As he pads barefoot into the kitchen, he feels feverish. Images of Kinsley's naked body invade his thoughts, and he has an overwhelming desire for sexual release. He lengthens his stride to get through the kitchen, following the smell of sugar, cherries, and jasmine into the living room.

He closes the gap between him and her in five strides and grabs her from behind, crushing her up against him. Kinsley had been expecting the magic to take over Carter's sensibilities, and make him relaxed, interested, and willing. She wiggles until he loosens his grip on her and turns to face him, bringing her arms up over her head and taking her shirt off in the process. Hungrily, they paw at each other, their mouths pressed together as they work each other's pants down.

Engrossed in each other and their lust, they don't hear the front door open, or Kori enter the house.

Kinsley, with her lips flattened against Carter's, has her head tipped to the side. She sees a shadow move and pulls away from Carter long enough to see Kori crossing the living room with determined steps, fists clenched at her sides.

Kori's eyes are blinking fast, and red is creeping up her neck and onto her face, which is twisted with anger. She looks crazed.

Kinsley stands frozen, watching Kori.

Carter, unaware that Kori has returned home, turns to see what's distracted Kinsley. He doesn't get time to register anything because Kori's balled-up hand hits his abs with all the power and anger Kori can put behind it. His breath explodes out of him in a loud grunt. He doubles over, gasping for air.

Kori, with flaring nostrils and a clenched jaw, wants to get her hands on Kinsley, but Carter is doubled over between them. Without breaking stride, Kori hooks her hands together, cups them over the back of Carter's neck and pulls him forward as she steps backward. He drops to the floor, groaning and gulping for air. Kori steps over him.

The moment she saw Kori in the room, Kinsley decided she wouldn't fight. Kori coming home adds to the scandal—malicious gossip, dishonour, and disgrace to the Ember Family—Kinsley wants to create after all. Fighting Kori in her own living room won't help Kinsley's cause, but letting Kori make a victim of her will. Kinsley is ready to get the same treatment as Carter, but Kori has made her own decisions as she crosses the room like an angry bull.

Clamping her right hand around Kinsley's left biceps, Kori yanks her forward. When Kinsley doesn't resist, Kori pulls her through the living room to the front door. She yanks the door open with her left hand and shoves Kinsley outside in the nude.

Kori slams and locks the door. Kinsley says nothing, and even now, Kori can hear no sounds from outside, no banging on the door, no calling out for her clothes. Just silence.

Kori stomps past the living room and looks in at Carter. He's curled up on the floor facing away from her. His back is moving like he's breathing hard. She dismisses him and continues to the bedroom. Her face pinched in disgust, she sweeps things into a suitcase and carry-on with little thought and marches out the house without a word. There's no sign of Kinsley.

Chapter 4

Kinsley shifts into human form in front of her house. Nobody is walking down the sidewalk, and no children are outside playing; it's uncanny how empty the street is. If nosy neighbours are peeking out their windows, Kinsley doesn't know or care as she strolls up to her front door.

Magic comes alive on her fingertips when she sees the door is ajar. Without breaking stride, she kicks it with the bottom of her foot and releases a magical net into the room, counting on its sticky threads to capture anyone in the area. She chases the net with feelers of magic but doesn't wait to enter. The net disintegrates when it lands on the floor in an empty tangle. The magic feelers didn't sense any life forms.

Kinsley's nostrils flare. There's nobody in the house, but the anesthetic-type stink of formaldehyde is present. Dolion's fascination with embalming isn't well-known, so the fact that Kinsley knows about it infuriates him. His scent is subtle, suggesting the smell is thinning out, so it's been a while since he was here. Dolion himself came to hunt her.

Despite her nudity, Kinsley's clammy, and there's a tremor in her hands. Few things cause her to display a fear response, but the torturous acts Dolion threatened to do to her if he caught her are terrifying. The abuse he's capable of . . . Her legs feel weak. Her parent's bodies drift to the forefront of her mind, and she wonders, not for the first time, if there is a connection between them and Dolion, and between their murders and The Society of the Blood Wind. The pain of loss grips her heart. They weren't the best parents, but they were the ones she knew and, in their own way, they loved her. *What would my life have been like to grow up with love?* She cuts her thoughts off. Her lips curl with disgust at her open display of weakness.

"Not if I get you first, old man," she hisses into the silence of her empty house.

She pulls her shoulders back, thrusts her chest out, and arches her chin up. A self-satisfied smile steals over her features as she remembers challenging Dolion in front of several members of The Society of the Blood Wind. The memory makes her feel bigger and stronger. She knows it was the split-second moment of Dolion's astonishment that kept her alive and gave her a moment to flee. She didn't run away so much as she disappeared to train and plan—now she's back to prevail, one step at a time. Kinsley can't help repeating the words that set him against her, the words that have become a part of her aspirations. "I will never be *just* a member of The Society when I can be its ruler."

For now, she has finished her time in Lindsay. She dresses and leaves, unwilling to risk Dolion's return. She needs to set the next part of her plan in motion, with a slight alteration since she likely isn't pregnant, and Kori found out about the affair before Kinsley wanted her to.

Before leaving town, Kinsley has one last thing to do. She baits a couple of henchmen from The Society of the Blood Wind by letting them see her. Because she's on Dolion's hate list, and therefore kill list, her physical appearance would be well known to those who are loyal followers. She waits for recognition to cross their features and then bolts so they'll chase her. She shifts where they'll see her and flies at a height that leaves her visible but out of range for any kind of magical attack they might throw. She suspects they aren't very strong in the magics since they don't use magic on her when they realize who she is, but she can't be sure. They may have been too surprised to react fast enough.

When the two burly men jump into a black SUV to give chase instead of shifting, Kinsley wonders if they're

Spellbinders at all. Even though all Spellbinders can shift, it's something that develops with age. So, there's the slim possibility they haven't mastered shapeshifting yet. None of it matters for the plan Kinsley has created, though. She sets a steady flight pace, leading them to the location she chose for the *accident* she's staging. She speeds up to get a bit more distance before flying around a corner and transforming into human form partway down the darkened one-way street. She glances between her wristwatch and the intersection at the far end of the road. If everything goes as planned, a second vehicle should enter the street behind her—which is the proper direction for this one-way.

Kinsley placed a call to Damien Casimir before baiting the henchmen. Damien is a well-known opposition to The Society of the Blood Wind. He hasn't aligned with the Ember family, but he shares several of their beliefs about Spellbinder and normie relationships. He runs a close second to the Embers in terms of power and influence within the Spellbinder community, but his methods of resistance are unpredictable and violent. The Society of the Blood Wind hasn't killed Damien because he's too public; his death would draw suspicion and unwanted attention to The Society. For these reasons, and because Damien's a threat to Kinsley's plans, she called him. She used the lure of a joint effort to damage The Society of the Blood Wind's reputation. He should arrive any minute.

Kinsley forms a tennis-ball-sized explosion orb and waits for the black SUV to turn the corner. The screech of braking tires precedes the physical appearance of the SUV, which is travelling in the wrong direction.

She's positioned almost in the middle of the street. Given that it's a single-lane with no sidewalks—flanked by the walls of businesses—Kinsley doesn't have any margin for error. She releases the orb as the SUV is still cornering. It hits the front left corner of the vehicle, lifting it three feet off the ground, on the front side, higher on the impact side, and slams it back down.

The back end of the SUV fishtails and crashes into the brick on the right side of the alley. The grating sounds of metal rubbing across brick as the vehicle grinds to a stop would have deafened Kinsley if she hadn't protected her hearing with a weave of magic. Since this explosion orb doesn't create shock waves, she doesn't need protection from the blast pressure, which is the point of this orb. The energy of the explosion is controlled by the magic in a way that doesn't cause energy to be transmitted outward.

The air is gritty with dust from the SUV colliding with the brick, and there's the stink of heated metal, burnt rubber, melting plastic, and lingering smoke. She stalks toward the unmoving SUV, focused on the two men inside. She cranks the driver's side door open. Neither of the men is moving, unconscious from the crash. Grabbing the driver, she yanks him out and lets him drop to the ground with a thud.

The passenger is slumped forward as Kinsley climbs into the driver's seat. With her hand on the back of his head, she wastes no time sinking a powerful jolt orb into his skull. The impact kills him. This isn't the death she wanted to give this man. He deserves an honourable death, like a warrior dying in battle, but she has to make it look like he died from a head injury caused by the crash while still leaving a residue of magic. The normie police need to see one thing, and any Spellbinder that turns up on the scene needs to see another.

Headlights round the corner at the opposite end of the street and slow down as she exits the SUV. A dark-coloured Jeep Gladiator creeps toward her. Quickly she sends a bolt of magic from her left hand into the SUV driver's chest where he lies in the road, stopping his heart. His body arches up, and as the magic dies out, it drops. From her right hand, she throws another explosion orb at the Jeep that has now slowed to a stop directly in front of the SUV. It hits the front section of the vehicle closer to the passenger's side, jarring it up and down in a crunch and bang of plastic, metal, and rubber.

The explosion orbs make both vehicles look like they crashed into each other. Between the vehicles, the ground is littered with bits of plastic, glass, and debris. The assumption by the normie police will be that the driver of the SUV turned the wrong way on a one-way street, causing a collision that killed the passenger in the SUV.

Damien leaps out of the Jeep. "What the fuck?" he hollers.

Kinsley ignores him, and she turns away. She squats down like she's examining the dead man. Waiting for Damien to move around the open door of the Jeep, she removes a Smith and Wesson 642 .38 Special from her ankle holster. It's a smooth, comfortable weight in her hand, even if normie firearms aren't a Spellbinder's weapon of choice.

Damien's angry footfalls stop behind her. Before he can speak, she turns. Remaining in her crouch, she shoots upward, releasing three of the five rounds. He staggers, grabbing at his chest. His eyes are wide, and his mouth is opening and closing, but no recognizable words are coming out as he stumbles and falls to the ground.

Kinsley shrugs and turns back to the dead SUV driver. She positions the Smith and Wesson to give the appearance that it tumbled from his hand. She stands, removing a second .38 Special from a holster at the small of her back and fires a round between his eyes. *Just another job.* She places the second gun by Damien. The iron smell of blood wafts from his body, and she crinkles her nose at him. *Weak.*

She doesn't care how well the facts match with the staged crime. The normie police aren't her concern, and they'll never connect her with any of this. No cameras, no prints on the guns or dead guys, and she won't be at the scene when the police arrive—the exception being Constable Carter Legand's arrival.

She can hear sirens. Between the noise from the explosion orbs and the gunfire, someone was bound to call. Kinsley knows Carter is working. She confirmed it before she visited the dispatch centre to plant magic suggestions in the dispatcher's minds. Her plan requires Carter to arrive on the scene first, and with the dispatcher's *help,* he will. She also needed to control the flow of information about Kori finding her and Carter having an affair. With Kinsley's limited time, using the dispatchers for this as well just made sense, and it didn't add any extra strain to the mind manipulation she was already exposing them to. She rolled tonight's scheme, unexpected as it was, into one event. *Fast thinking, Kinsley.*

Kinsley moves to the wall in front of the SUV and magically marks it with two long horizontal flames that resemble abstract hands releasing swirls. The symbol— The Society of the Blood Wind logo—will let any Spellbinder that shows up know there's a connection between these deaths and The Society. *The Society's long-reaching hands were bound to get them in trouble one day.* Kinsley smirks as she surveys the scene she's created.

A police car jerks to a stop at the intersection of the street behind the SUV. It's angled so that the in-car camera, if it's on, will be recording the wall. Kinsley launches a confusion orb as soon as the driver's side door opens. It's Carter, but she knew it would be. Since the policy is one cop in the car, he's alone. The confusion orb makes Carter's senses a chaotic mishmash. If that were all Kinsley had planned for him, he'd remain tired and uncertain when the effects wore off, but she has more lined up for him.

She moves toward him, unhurried. She stays away from the front half of the police car to be sure she isn't caught on video. The wail of sirens is moving closer, but still far enough away that she's confident in her timeline. She watches him. He squeezes his eyes shut, shakes his head from side to side, and scrubs his ears with his hands. Kinsley angles her body and drives her elbow into Carter's face, knocking him unconscious. A warmth spreads through her, and she feels light and happy as she unzips his pants.

She leans in, her voice low, and whispers, "You'll have no memory of arriving on the scene or anything that happened here." She nips his ear. "It was good, Carter."

Straightening, she produces what looks like a cherry wood lipstick tube from a cargo pocket on her pants. It's a holder for sewing needles, and she has a special one for Carter. She holds the needle between her teeth, careful not to poke herself with it. The tip of the needle is black like fire charred it, and there's a grey fog swirling around it. She puts the tube back in her pocket and uses her left hand to hold his pants open around the zipper. She wiggles her fingers into the flap on the front of his underwear, exposing flesh. With her right hand, Kinsley takes the needle and jabs his penis with it. The magic coating the needle's point is a hex of impotence, obsession, and lunacy.

She flicks the needle into the sewer drain before zipping Carter's pants back up. "Without the cure for this hex, Carter, you'll slip slowly into madness. Deeper and deeper until there's no way out. You'll be preoccupied with your prick and fixated on how to rehabilitate it." Kinsley shrugs one shoulder up and pulls her lips back, surveying him.

"Why?" she says, like Carter is asking her. Her voice

is venomous. "Because I hate the Embers, and you married one. Because you failed to give me what I need, a baby. And because this is bigger than us."

A police car is coming down the street toward them. Kinsley shifts and flies out of town.

Acknowledgments

Big thanks to NaNoWriMo 2023, for providing me with the accountability I need to turn my outline for the last book in The Ember Files into a rough draft.

A shout out to Laura—my editor for The Ember Files series—for challenging me to look at my manuscripts from different perspectives, and for challenging me to grow as a writer. Your enthusiasm and skill as an editor ignited a spark to start my editing journey. Thank you.

I can't thank my husband and my sons enough for their patience when I attached myself to my laptop for days on end, writing and editing. Without your support, this journey wouldn't have been the same.

Book Club Reading Guide

1. Which character bothered you the most?
2. If you were making a film adaptation of this book, who would you cast for the characters?
3. What did you think of the character's names? Did they match their personalities?
4. How does the setting impact the story?
5. What are your thoughts on what happens to the characters after the end of the book?
6. How would you describe the pace of the plot?
7. If you could change how the story ended, what would you have happened?
8. How did you feel right after you finished reading this book?

www.ingramcontent.com/pod-product-compliance
Lightning Source LLC
Chambersburg PA
CBHW061153210726
48294CB00006B/1661